Falling
from Trees

"Like the best science fiction, Mike Fiorito's collection of short stories is both familiar and fanciful, engaging the reader with memorable imagery. In clear and evocative prose, he communicates worlds strange and sad, hopeful, and poignant, brilliant and mysterious."

— Rebecca Bauman, Ph.D., Associate Professor of Italian, Dept. of Modern Languages and Cultures, Fashion Institute of Technology, SUNY

"Fiorito is an accomplished writer, and in this collection of short stories he creates a series of intriguing vignettes, which together make up far more than the sum of their parts. The atmospheres conjured up stay with you long after reading, by turns wistful, illogical, and deeply human. A diverting book with a unique flavor."

— Nikki Wyrd, editor of the *Psychedelic Press Journal*

"Fiorito's *Falling from Trees* is a collection of short stories that revolve around one theme—the relationship with the other, with what's 'different' and troubles our balance. But it is precisely this 'diversity' that saves us because what apparently separates us is what unites us. The important thing is to know, as one of the protagonists says, that "everything is relative", even the distance between Earth and other planets. Fiorito uses a surreal and dream style to outline his characters, children who draw alone and see "the immortality of yellow", or aliens that bring special gifts to humanity: first and foremost, the meaning of life. And so, thanks to their gifts, all of us finally "have a purpose" and discover "that the universe is made of music."

— Maria Rosa Cutrufelli, author of *The Woman Outlaw*

"What makes Mike Fiorito's *Falling from Trees* fantastic aren't elements of the fantastic—aliens and intergalactic travel, miracles and magic—but, rather, what the interconnected stories show us about relationships. Plucking familiar pangs of human emotion out of a starry sea of the strange and unfamiliar, Fiorito teaches us we need not look across the universe for universal truth. His characters are as genuine and relatable as creation is vast and mysterious, and through them, we can come to understand our place in it a little bit better."

> — Chad Frame, Director of the Montgomery County Poet Laureate Program

"In *Falling from Trees*, Mike Fiorito dreams lucid of a future where alien contact saves humanity from itself. Telepathic communication, benevolent corporal possession, music, and poetry are portals to the secret language of the universe. Treading the trails of futurists such as Aldous Huxley and Buckminster Fuller, Mike Fiorito envisions a utopia where there is no need for greed, hunger, or war. These extra temporal tales give an inkling of what could be if we are open to the beauty behind the stars."

> — Mike Cobb, Writer

"It is refreshing to read a collection of related sci-fi stories that is not dystopian in its message. But this is exactly what author Mike Fiorito has brilliantly created. The language is as accessible and relatable as the message: the humble inherit the earth and join their alien brethren in a world of song and understanding where rivers have song and everything is made of space spice, the oceans sing, the trees record time...There is a timeless quality and interconnectedness to *Falling from Trees*, a oneness of love and song posited by Mr. Fiorito as the eventual awakening to a shared and joyous destiny. *Falling from Trees* is a book of hope above all else, a spiritual journey among the stars."

— Ryan Quinn Flanagan, Author of *The Road to Hell is Paved with Writers*

"Being a masterful weaver of words & teller of tales, Mike's stories subtly draw you in and before you know it, take a hold of you. Bridging the philosophical / cosmic side of life to the theological / nostalgic side, believe me when I say the ride Mike Fiorito will take you on in this collection will be colorful, insightful and ultimately you'll come away a better person for experiencing it."

— Johnny Olson, Founder/Chief Editor/Creative Director, Mad Swirl

"Fiorito's astute imagination carries us to places that, on the surface, seem identifiable, but instead create a enough of a dissonance for us to realize we are out of the realm of what we know, at once uncomfortable in our ease and able to conceptualize all of the vagaries this life of ours holds. An absolutely luminous collection of stories that adds yet another layer of surreality to the times in which we find ourselves."

— Michelle Reale, author of *Season of Subtraction*

"Fiorito's stories in *Falling from Trees* are a magical reminder of the writings of a number of my favorite writers including Jorges Borges, Italo Calvino, Philip K Dick and Ray Bradbury."

— Anthony Peake, author of *The Hidden Universe*

Falling from Trees

Mike Fiorito

Apprentice
House Press
Loyola University Maryland

First Edition

Hardcover ISBN: 978-1-62720-332-6
Paperback ISBN: 978-1-62720-333-3
Ebook ISBN: 978-1-62720-334-0

Printed in the United States of America

Design: Mackenzie Britt
Promotion plan: Eric Boyd
Managing editor: Kelley Chan
Cover Art: Pat Singer http://www.patsingerart.com

Published by Apprentice House Press

Apprentice
House Press
Loyola University Maryland

Apprentice House Press
Loyola University Maryland
4501 N. Charles Street
Baltimore, MD 21210
410.617.5265 • 410.617.2198 (fax)
www.ApprenticeHouse.com
info@ApprenticeHouse.com

Contents

Dedicated to my wife, Arielle,
and my sons, Thelonious and Travis.

The more enlightened our houses are,
the more their walls ooze ghosts.
- Italo Calvino

Preface

Falling from Trees is a collection of tales that explore the possibilities of sentient knowledge and the evolution of consciousness. The stories are related and connect to each as much through time portals as through the arteries of the heart. You might say they are concerned with the meaning of love. Can consciousness extend beyond the confines of our everyday world by plumbing the infinite places of the heart?

The stories in *Falling from Trees* invite us to investigate our thinking. They are not cynical tales; in fact, the stories celebrate our potential salvation. Perhaps the answers have always been where our eyes meet at the tip of our noses. Perhaps the portholes across the galaxies are activated by birdsong. And, to discover these invisible conveyances, we must change the way we imagine ourselves in the universe. No spaceships. No thermonuclear combustion engines. Instead, perhaps the yellow of a dandelion contains enough knowledge to transport us to every place at any time.

Foreword

In these tumultuous times, science fiction can be either comforting or provocative. Mike Fiorito's *Falling from Trees* is both. His stories depict the alien race that rescues humanity through imagery, color, and sound, transcending the distance between its planet and Earth.

The collection begins with "Climbing Time" where the aliens reach out to individuals with Asperger's, communicating with them in vivid, wordless dreams. Another common theme is the disastrous impact of climate change. In a prescient irony, the interconnected "Pale Leviathan" and "Tomorrow's Ghost" present the fierceness of the sun invading the characters' cooled home and the claustrophobia of the world where soon children will, as in our world, be forced to attend school remotely. The ending of "Tomorrow's Ghost" blends provocation and comfort in a particularly striking way. Other stories follow the enigmatic alien Smith, a "word person" rather than a numbers person, through believable, mysterious encounters with humans. A change of pace story portrays the possibility of romance between an astronomer and a magician, both of Italian descent.

Those of you whose experience with science fiction is limited to a few episodes of *Star Trek* should take a chance on Fiorito's stories. They showcase the genre's possibilities for character as well as world-building that emphasizes imagery, color, and sound over technology, especially military technology.

-Marianne Szlyk, author of *Poetry en Plein Air*

Climbing Time

I've been diagnosed as having Asperger's. This means that I act like a robot sometimes. This is what other people tell me. This is also why I have extraordinary computational skills. I can calculate numbers in my head in an instant. I can determine on what day your birthday fell ten years ago. It's like I can walk down numbered pathways in my mind, as if they were a grid. I can get sunk into a project or a problem for days.

Even though I worked on a retail floor of a computer store, I was an astronomy enthusiast. When the aliens came, that all changed.

We detected a signal coming from ninety-five million light-years away. We were watching. I was watching.

We learned that an intelligent species launched a high-powered pulse across a swath of space, hoping someone else was watching, listening.

I started to have dreams.

To build the future the aliens messaged Asperger's, people who could come closest to understanding their computational concepts. Asperger's heard the music, had dreams, visions which were coded instructions. People in charge, the leaders and scientists, were dumbfounded by the aliens. Former post office workers, cab drivers, became the liaisons to the ETs. The humble inherited the earth.

The aliens conveyed environmentally clean energy solutions, new medical technologies and practices to us. These gifts offered immense prosperity and promised the end of war.

No one ever met them or saw them. They sent directed telepathic messages from far beyond our solar system. The messages came like wind over the earth. Sometimes the messages arrived as music. Sometimes the messages came in dreams. Images of the oceans pouring over the earth, their blue waters spilling and crashing. Whales, sharks. Schools of colorful fish. Rivers, their waters like a runaway train, drowning the mind. Millions of suns on fire.

Only some people, people like me, could follow the patterns. Sometimes the music sounded like Bach or a computer speaking a combination of Finnish and twinkling synth tones. The sounds could be like crying or singing. Or laughter. Sometimes messages were conveyed in colors that could shoot an arrow of understanding into the brain. I could be eating breakfast or in the shower. I'd have to make rushed notations in soap, so I could hold the ideas.

The Asperger's were grouped. Some were designated on the environmental teams, relaying harvesting methods for solar, wind and galactic core energy. Some were designated for information technology projects. Some, like me, were astronomers. We learned that many of the principal concepts were amazingly simple and common across disciplines. The scientific principles could be sung like lullabies. The basic ideas were similar in theme; each discipline offered a different melody of the same theme. I'd sometimes wake up with tears on my cheeks or, at other times, laughing hysterically. I'd jot down dashes and figures on a pad. I'd heard that some people painted, some used hand gestures like they were conducting a symphony.

Some danced.

I wondered what was in it for the aliens. They answered

me in a dream. I dreamt of humans and animals walking the earth. I glimpsed the entire span of evolution. The mutation of flesh, the wholesale murder of species upon species. The fragility of the flesh in a universe of pulsars, collapsing stars.

In the dream, the aliens revealed their hope. They were interested in learning how our brain structures, which emerged from two-eyed, two-legged, ten-fingered species, developed and applied math concepts. They were also curious about why we were so receptive to music. The basis of all complex thinking was rooted in music. But the human capacity for understanding music far outpaced our understanding of the underlying science. How could this be so, they wondered? We seemed to them like furious idiots, sophisticated yet savage.

We are now all working together, led by Asperger's, like me. The politicians, the scientists, the academics - all learning from the Asperger's. We've begun to truly cooperate. There is nothing to fight for anymore. We all have health, adequate space and energy needs for our homes. We have all become scientists and composers. We all have a purpose.

The oceans are clearing. The forests are returning. The filth that gas, coal and oil created, which has polluted the earth, has greatly diminished. The skies are clear again. And the war mongers? No one would follow tyrants anymore. Tyrants need followers. People seem content. They see hope. We feel in our bones that this will last. We even pray now. We love.

We are now part of a network with sentient beings from distant galaxies as well. We are learning the great catalog of songs. The songs contain everything. The songs are a combination of loving kindness wrapped in the structure of how things work. Bizarre. The songs are poems.

It turns out that the universe is made of music. Its secrets are trapped in the melodies of ocean water, in the rushing of waterfalls.

The Love of a Dandelion

Even as a boy, he felt yellow; even just looking at it on a page, his skin became heated by its invisible rays. In school, he drew suns with fiery light rays shooting off its surface.

"You should draw something else, Colin," his teacher, Mrs. Lipshitz, said. "There are trees, grass hills and houses, too."

"I like suns. I draw suns. I love their light. They make me happy," he said, his green eyes sparkling with faint yellow streaks.

She tried to understand, nodding her head, looking down at the drawing on his desk. The other kids drew stick figures and bent trees, but his suns were explosive, like he'd visited their surfaces. His suns boasted fiery lakes, passionately real and alive.

"What an imagination you have," said Mrs. Lipshitz.

"I draw what I see," he replied.

"And what do you see?" she asked.

"I see the immortality of yellow. Even suns and flowers come and go. But yellow is forever."

Years later, in math class, he'd look at the blackboard, admiring the elegant manner of quadratic equations. He solved the problems easily, as if with each stroke of his pencil he produced the answer instantly. After doing his assignments in class, he drew pictures of suns, of dandelions and of sunflowers with ink pens and magic markers.

"Have you finished your work?" asked Mr. Murphy, his math teacher. Mr. Murphy was a big man and coach of the basketball team, too. He didn't like boys who drew.

"I did the work," said Colin, turning the paper around to show Mr. Murphy. His handwriting was impeccable. "I did it in a few minutes." The classroom was silent except for the other kids' pencils scratching the paper.

"You're not cheating, Colin?"

Colin looked at him blankly. They both knew this wasn't true.

"I don't like you to bring markers to class."

"But I do the lessons. I learn more from doing my drawings."

The next day, Mr. Murphy sent Colin to the school guidance counselor, Mr. Thomas Lopez.

Colin liked Mr. Lopez as soon as he walked in the door. Mr. Lopez wore a bright yellow bow tie and high-water pants that didn't reach his feet.

Mr. Lopez reached out his hand and said, "Please call me Thomas."

"Nice to meet you, Thomas," said Colin.

"You are gaining quite a reputation with the beautiful drawings you make."

Colin nodded his head, saying thank you.

"Mr. Murphy says that you disturb the class."

"I do the work he assigns. He doesn't really get the problems he has us solve."

Mr. Lopez wrote on his notepad.

"But why do you bring markers to the class?"

"I like to draw." He looked at Mr. Lopez's tie.

"Do you mind if I draw your tie?"

6

"No, please, go ahead," said Mr. Lopez. "What do you feel when you draw?" asked Mr. Lopez.

Colin stopped drawing and fixed his eyes on Mr. Lopez.

"What if I told you that I can leap on the yellow of the suns I draw and travel great distances? What if I told you that people bother themselves with figuring out math problems about the speed of light, when what they really need to do is to learn how to communicate with color?"

"This is a little out of my league, Colin. I'm only a counselor." Mr. Lopez wrote vigorously in his notebook.

"But you know about these things. You know that it would take one hundred years traveling at the speed of light just to get to the nearest star."

"I've seen the movies," said Mr. Lopez.

"You think I'm crazy?" asked Colin. "Is that what you're writing in your notepad?"

"It does sound a little outrageous," said Mr. Lopez, now putting down his notepad.

Colin picked up his paper to show Mr. Lopez the tie he'd drawn. Mr. Lopez saw that the tie was brilliantly yellow, exploding with shades of orange yellow. The yellow tones reminded Mr. Lopez of the summer dress his recently deceased mother had worn in a photo on his desk at home. Had Colin seen into his heart and depicted his feelings?

As Mr. Lopez gazed at the drawing, he tried to conceal how affected he was.

"So, you're a terrific artist," said Mr. Lopez, rubbing his cheek with the knuckle of his index finger.

"What if I told you that you could travel to another galaxy?" asked Colin.

"I would find it interesting," said Mr. Lopez. "How could you know about these kinds of things? You're in high school."

"Then how come I knew that drawing would remind you of your mother."

Mr. Lopez collected himself on his chair.

"What do scientists know anyway? They think travelling in capsules is the answer to space travel."

"And what do you think, Colin?"

"Our scientists are trying to understand space travel through understanding math. If you could ride yellow, you could transport yourself to any place in the universe in seconds. By comparison, math is like riding a bicycle to Mars."

"This is very interesting, but how can you prove any of this?"

"What can you prove?" asked Colin.

"I can prove that the earth travels around the sun and that the moon travels around the earth," said Mr. Lopez.

"You need other people's books and research to prove these things. It wouldn't be your proof. In the future, the very idea of intergalactic travel will be something everyone can do."

"And how will they do that?"

"I don't know yet. But I think people will be able to navigate time and space through some mechanism, some door. We will discover that there is no beginning and end. That God is so unbounded He doesn't have to exist. When we discover the love of a dandelion and have compassion for even the sun, we will arrive at these truths."

"How can you love a dandelion?"

"When you realize that the yellow of a dandelion is the door to the memory of your mother, you can love it."

The Thread

I was a high school teacher before they came. I'm not sure what I am now. They said they chose me because they needed cases to test. To make sure their experiments worked. Now I feel more like a Wax Museum custodian than anything else.

What I most recall is that it was a very regular night. Even the light grey sky outside my office window looked no different from the sky I'd seen many nights previously. Looking back now, I remember the extra shades of purple at twilight, but if it weren't for what followed, I wouldn't have noticed.

One minute I was preparing a lesson for the following day, when suddenly I felt dizzy. It was as if my thoughts began to echo. Then my body felt uncomfortable, like my arms and legs were being operated by someone else. Like there was another presence in my body. The presence moved down my chest into my waist and extended into my fingers and toes. Although I was disturbed by the strangeness of this experience, the feeling was not menacing. I felt very clear; in fact, my senses were extraordinarily powerful, as if colors were more vivid and my thinking was many times sharper. As I looked around the room, I was struck by my own lucidity. I knew now that my body had been occupied by another sentience. I knew it was a benevolent being. I felt enormous, like I was reclining across the solar system, my hands resting on Saturn and my feet stretched out all the way to Venus.

Then words began to form in my mind, words that I had not thought but which came to me. The words seemed to swell from a chorus of violin notes tickling my bone marrow.

Then something began to speak to me.

"I have come to tell you an urgent message." Each word was loving and sweet, like a soft whistle caressing my ear, my heart. It continued.

"The earth is on course with a detonation that is scheduled to demolish it almost momentarily. We have entered your physical form to assist in the mission to maintain life on this planet."

Oddly, I wasn't perturbed about what I was hearing.

"We must now transport all human life on Earth to a remote location, so that we can adjust the movement of the earth without wiping out the human race with climate and environmental upheavals."

Our conversation was less a voice in my head, but rather a flowing of sensations, words and images into my body. The way your body feels when the sounds of a cello vibrate your muscles. On the edge of each swell of music was a word or an idea which emerged from the tidal wave of pulsations. The presence continued.

"We have preserved all human DNA, neurological configurations and physiological data in HoloByte datagrams. We have monitored the three-dimensional data fields of all humans and have extensively detailed the records; we have mapped out the perceptual and mental fields down to the last reckoning thought of each person. And now we will realign the cities and Earth's natural surface down to a blade of grass. Our reconstruction process could take a few hundred human years, but no one will know. Scientists may recognize a slight shift in the distribution of galaxies, and they will naturally speculate on their findings. They will develop theories but will be unable to solve the mystery for centuries. But it will pass unnoticed by the general public, only trickling down to them in an obscure theory."

The presence continued.

"Humans will not notice the hundreds of years that will have passed in between their conscious moments. About one thousand years ago we did a similar experiment in the permanence of consciousness; it went completely undetected, although some people had, what they claimed to be, spiritual experiences. Naturally, spiritual experiences are not scientifically provable.

"I am sorry to inform you, but as you will participate in the mission, we must wipe your memories afterwards. It will not hurt, and we will make sure that you are comfortably restored. You will have experienced a shock, and then you will wake being unable to remember the moment we contacted you."

The presence stopped speaking.

Suddenly, I was looking down at the earth from a pocket of white space, floating in the darkness.

Then I observed something so terrible I can hardly describe it. I saw the earth being hit by a pulverizing force. The explosion sent the earth hurtling along into particles rushing away from each other.

The earth was gone now. There were chunks of rocks moving around in slow motion, spinning from top to bottom.

The presence said that human minds were saved, but all physical records of humanity and all human bodies were destroyed. All our lives, history and culture were now trapped on an electronic device. The entirety of the earth, they said, could be brought back - with some work. The idea of everything hanging by a thread was somehow both sad and terrifying.

I could feel the presence crying in pain along with me.

Twilight

The thing he missed most was the sound of birdsong.

After the change, you no longer heard birds. You might see birds high in the sky, now and again, far from humans, as if too frightened to come near. But you didn't hear them. You couldn't hear anything. There was a ringing that droned in his ears, but he wasn't sure if that was the after effect of the noise the explosion made or if was just something he heard. There weren't any trees either. The sky was barren, a stark grey pallor filled the sky.

He walked along the shore. The ocean water didn't come in great crashing waves like before. The water moved like thick petroleum. He drank the water. Even if it killed him, he had to drink it so as not to die anyway.

He'd been walking alone for at least a year. He'd seen a few people. He met one man a few months ago who was looking for his wife. He spent a night with the man. They ate a raccoon together on a spit, cooking above a great fire. The man's eyes were streaked red. He spoke in whispers.

"I used to be farmer," he said. "Before the change." No one referred to what happened.

"She can't be far from here," the farmer said.

"Do you think she made it out alive?"

"My wife made it out," the farmer replied sternly. "She'd called me the night before and said she was taking a plane back from the Midwest to the coast."

The man imagined the plane evaporating in the sky, turning into a splotch of water in midair.

He listened to the farmer, chewing on the gamey raccoon meat. It wasn't tasty, but it would keep him alive. He licked his fingers to savor every bit of the meat. This kind of meal didn't come around too often. When you saw something move, you killed it and ate it to stay alive.

"She made it out alright. I've walked up and down this coast about ten miles in each direction. I know I'll find her. She wouldn't leave me. She couldn't live without me."

The man watched his friend tell his story, the moisture of his eyes glowing in the firelight. He missed his own wife and two boys, but he knew he would never see them again. They died in the explosion, along with almost everyone and everything else. He remembered the heat when the sky went brilliantly white. There was a loud boom that drew everything into an eye in the sky and then a deep silence. Then the heat came pouring from the sky, like a great oven door had been opened. The heat burned his nose and throat, like he'd gulped flames. He saw bodies vaporize, some splattered onto walls, their silhouettes outlining arms and legs reaching out in fear. For days afterward he saw only dead things on the streets and wondered why he hadn't died. Why should he have survived? He had been in a garage, working late into the night. The metal garage door was only slightly open. He worked by an artificial lamp, listening to the radio. He liked the old music.

But some had survived, like this farmer. They wandered around in shock, frightened and unable to believe what had had happened. The earth was annihilated. A giant clang had emptied the planet.

When the man left in the morning, they shook hands.

"I hope you find your wife," he said.

"Are you looking for anyone?" the farmer asked.

The man didn't reply. They didn't exchange names. Why should they? No one needed names. Everything was nameless, even the things on the earth. It was just a matter of time before he'd be gone, too. He knew it. There wasn't any point in pushing too hard. He walked to walk. He looked up at the dark sky and wondered what the point of the history of life on the planet had been. He wondered why we'd evolved from monkeys. Human beings were just too stupid to survive. Millions upon millions of lives since the dinosaurs. We came this far, reached out into space and then folded in and blew ourselves up.

None of it mattered anymore. But what he missed most were the Sunday nights walking with his family to the park. He loved the twilight. The sound of the birds, finches and sparrows chirping in the trees. So many trees. Oak, maple and locust trees. And the cloying smells of flowers. His wife showed him the flowers. Pulling a bud off a flower, she handed it to him.

"Smell it," she said.

He smelled it, almost begrudgingly, his mind preoccupied with work. Despite his initial resistance, he loved the way flowers smelled. This time he even pulled a few buds off the tree himself. He looked down the wide street that led to the park. There were gigantic oaks, some more than a hundred years old, their leaves gleaming in the sunlight. It wasn't clear why trees, flowers and sunlight could be so refreshing.

He remembered the last time he looked way down at the row of houses. Some of the houses were mansions at one time. Rich merchants from the city had built their mansions on these pretty streets. Each house was designed differently, each a different color. Most of the houses had gardens, showing off tulips, dandelions and lilacs. The very last time he took in the view and breathed the air, he looked up at the sun, now setting over the trees. He was happy to be alive, happy to have this moment. He heard birds twittering from high up in a tree. They were nesting in the branches, out of sight.

He thought to himself: This could be the last time.

Tiny Blue Oceans

It was becoming hard to deny that he could suffocate as he sat motionless in the slight capsule floating between the earth and the moon.

"Captain Collins, can you read me?" the voice from Command Control said.

"Yes, I hear you Command."

"We're working on the booster engine, Captain."

"And?"

"Still work to do, Captain."

"Well, listen, I want to get home before Christmas." It was October.

"Yes sir, Captain," he said, followed by a long static sound. Then, "We want to get you home in time to cut the turkey."

No use in panicking, yet. Maintain cool under pressure. Losing the booster jets wasn't the first thing to go wrong. A few weeks ago, one of the communications antennae failed. Collins had to perform extravehicular repair on the module. It took days, painstakingly working with Command Control to remove the fried interface card and install a new one. It was a close call and lucky that the backup worked. Losing the antenna could have cut off all communication with Command Control, not to mention cutting off the flow of images and data.

While Command Control worked on the engine, Collins busied himself with preparations for landing, reviewing the landing protocols. There were several precise steps that had to be executed in sequence. One mistake could cost him the mission, or worse, his life.

"Captain?"

"Yes, Command."

"We're going to go offline for a bit, working in the lab to reproduce the problem. Signing off for now."

He heard a long static noise again, like a sound particle bouncing off the blue round surface of the earth, then racing toward the ship like a high-pitched scream.

He studied the landing protocol manual even though he knew it by heart. He had always been good at memorizing things, and he possessed an intuitive sense of how things worked. That's why he had been picked for this mission. Working with his father repairing antique Chevys was just as important as his engineering degree from Cal Tech. He could solve any problem, not just math problems. But he wasn't as good with people. People were way more complicated; they didn't come with manuals. People's minds didn't always follow the dictates of logic. He drifted back remembering how his wife got upset at him a few months ago for trying to fix her problems instead of just listening.

"This is just standard scientific procedure. You're going to be okay," he said, when the results from the reproductive tests indicated that she might be infertile.

"Why don't you just say that you don't understand how I feel?" she asked.

"Because I want to remain hopeful," he said. "We don't have a problem, yet."

"Are you saying that I'm not hopeful?"

He didn't reply.

"It's not all about you. Sometimes you're an insensitive asshole."

He was shocked. He was only trying to remain positive.

Then she banished him from the bedroom to sleep on the couch. Even on the couch he couldn't stop thinking about how she overreacted. He didn't feel like he had done anything wrong. He wished he could understand her feelings, so he could tell her how to change. He loved her, though he only told her once, the night they were married. She cried for at least an hour; then they made love. *I should tell her more often*, he thought at the time. She was like a volcano that night. But I can't. I just can't. It doesn't come out of my damned mouth.

As his mind raced, he looked up from the screen and out the window. There it was: Earth. Everything going on in the world is happening there now. War, joy, defeat, rape, murder, sadness and peace. All at once, everywhere. My father is dead in the ground somewhere down there, along with his father's father, all the way back to primates and beyond – to reptiles and small, wormy creatures – then just scum on the surface of a rock. The thought made him slightly lightheaded. Every car, river, mountain and house – it's all there on that one planet.

He marveled at the blue-white surface, how it was illuminated. It looked like a sanctuary from up here. Even nasty hurricanes cartwheeling across oceans looked placid. Gigantic nighttime thunderstorms flashing and flaring for hundreds of miles along the equator appeared as light shows. And his wife was down there now, waiting for him. She was probably at the hospital, saving a heart patient at this very moment. Being one of the finest heart doctors in the Bay Area kept her a busy woman. Command Control probably hadn't yet alerted her to the possibility that the ship could be stranded. They hadn't yet reached that point yet. The point when saving him was futile. He put that out of his mind for now. For the moment he looked at the earth and felt thankful. Here in all this darkness, in this cold, empty spot, he could see that the blue planet was on fire with life. Here was a place teeming with creatures, with trees and flowers. Here was a place, despite the wars and the evils people commit, here survived all known human existence. This tiny, fragile, little sphere hurling through space.

"Captain?"

Then another long static hiss.

"Yes Command. I read you."

"Captain, we may have found something."

He looked at the clock. He knew they had about ten hours. After that the ship would not have enough oxygen for the trip back. He'd already used all the surplus tanks.

"Okay Command. Shoot."

Command Control directed him to the steps he had to take. He couldn't do all of this himself, though he wished he could. He had to rely on someone else. It infuriated him to rely on others.

Then a series of call and responses.

"A3?"

"Check," said the Captain.

"A1?"

"Check."

Command continued reading off check points. Then.

"A15-2."

"Failed."

"Repeat, Captain."

"Failed. The unit is not responding."

Now a hiss, then a long silence. Collins stared at the monitor. He felt a pulse of panic torque his spine, like an electronic whip had just sent a spark coiling through his body. He looked out the window at the blue planet. *If only I could just jump to you. There you are and here I am, stuck.*

"We'll keep trying, Riley."

"Roger that, Dalbert." For the first time there was a hint of despair in his voice.

"Hang in there, Riley." Command paused. "We're going to bring you home."

With nothing else to do, he worked his way over to the food cabinet, climbing on the array of bars that allowed him to move around in zero gravity without floating into walls.

Three hours passed.

"Captain Collins," he heard after he'd finished eating.

"Yes, sir."

"We have a surprise for you." The voice was interrupted, after ricocheting off the moon and bouncing back onto the earth, only to beam back to the ship.

"We can turn to video, if you'd like. Your wife, Natalie, is here."

Hearing his wife's name both comforted and frightened him. *I'm not sure if I want her to see me. But I need to see her.*

He looked at the clock. Time was running out.

He hit the mute button. He needed a few moments to collect himself.

"Okay, command. Switching to video."

"Riley, how are you doing up there?" she said, her voice cracking, trying to reign in her emotions.

"Hey, sweetie. See, it's just like any other Saturday working on the car."

"I know, honey," she said, wiping a tear from her eye.

"Still got a few tricks in the bag," he said for the both of them, even though he knew this was like reading last rites to him.

"Well, I've been at the hospital all day, working overtime," she said, "trying to keep my mind off of my husband flying around in space."

"That's good, honey. You're the best doctor they have."

"I don't know," she said, "but I never sleep well when I know you're out there."

"Falling asleep is what these guys are doing," he said, forcing a smile. "They better get on it."

"I know, I know, honey," she said, "they're all working hard for you. For us." Her eyes glimmered, even on the screen, the blue surfaces like the blue of the earth's oceans. He had never noticed that. The oceans flowed through her. She drank their waters, ate foods that were fed by their abundance. She was a living, breathing, intelligent creature that stepped out of the oceans and onto the shores.

"I love you," he finally said.

"I love you, too," she answered, her voice breaking up from crying and then splintering from interference. The "too" was digitized then stretched by a frequency pitch. The sound then broke into bits and bounced off the interior of the capsule.

"If anything happens to me up here," he said, "I want you to be okay. Everybody needs you," he said.

"You're going to be fine, Riley. They're going to get you home."

"Yes, they will," he said, transfixed by the blue of her eyes. She was made of wind and rain and of oceans and mud.

"I'm going to go now, Riley. I'll be back in a while. I love you," she said, getting up from the video monitor. She threw kisses at him, rubbing her eyes with the other hand.

"I love you, too," he said. The words sounded hollow in the capsule.

Now Riley stood looking at Dalbert. His eyes, too, sparkled with moisture. Riley realized that something was coming over him. He was seeing how much alike all people were, how all people are containers of water, breakable and soft.

"We have a few more tests to run, Riley," said Dalbert.

Riley looked at the clock. Not much time left. Numbers. Time. He calculated how much time they had before it was too late. All his life, he couldn't help adding, subtracting, deriving percentages. That's the way his mind worked. This little fact of calculation now made it clear that if they didn't solve the problem in the next two hours, he would surely die.

Simulacrum

Ever since St. Bernadette had a vision of Mary in the grotto, tourists came to Lourdes, some to be healed by its miracle.

Arriving by train in Lourdes, Roberto alighted onto the streets, now crowded with seekers from across the globe.

They came from all over the world, some on crutches, some in wheelchairs, some even on flat beds. They all came in quest of a miracle.

"You see this queue," said Genevieve, his French guide, pointing to the long line of people who waited to pass through the grotto. "They've come to touch the stone where Mary is said to have appeared." The line to enter the grotto seemed endless. Then there was a queue of people returning from the grotto, yet none seemed to be healed. And none of them looked disappointed either. Some were wheeled back on beds, their eyes looking heavenward. There was an ecstasy even in the failure of the enterprise. One elderly man clutched rosary beads close to his chest, his teeth chattering.

"Bernadette's father was put in prison after she told the local church about her visions," continued Genevieve, as men walked by holding full-sized crosses like a fleet of crusaders.

"She had over thirty visions," she added, hunching her shoulders and running her fingers through her straight, greasy hair. She sweated heavily in the August heat, her glasses misted from the humidity.

Nestled at the foothills of the Pyrenees, the sun mercilessly rained down in flames on Lourdes. The sun's rays stung Roberto's pale cheeks.

"Why did they imprison her father?" a German on the tour meekly asked.

"She threatened the authority of the church," Genevieve quickly replied. As she spoke, wayfarers rushed by holding banners proclaiming their church affiliations, as if sprung from out of the Middle Ages.

"Isn't it ironic that mystics and visionaries became the thorn in the side of the church?" she asked. No one ventured a reply.

Many of the visitors elected to not go inside the grotto and instead waited their turn at the fountain to bottle holy water. The holy water came from the spring that flowed inside the grotto. Roberto bottled some water to distribute as souvenirs for his family. They accepted the ideas of the church without struggle. He, however, suffered from doubts.

Genevieve continued her lecture on the Catholic leaders who assumed control of Lourdes, expanding it over the years and finally building the cathedral, the various sanctuaries, statues and fountains on the grounds.

"Do you believe that the grotto has miraculous powers?" Roberto blurted, the question escaping from his lips.

"Of course, I believe. That goes without saying," she said. "You're telling me that you don't feel anything sacred here?"

Roberto bowed his head out of embarrassment.

"You must have come for some reason," she said. "Or is it just intellectual curiosity?"

She paused then said, raising her voice, "Some people come to Lourdes merely to ridicule it. As if this is all a pathetic circus."

An English couple gave him a look of disgust. Roberto sunk back into the group, trying not to stand out. He took out a sandwich and quietly ate it as he looked on and listened.

The tour ended on a street next to the gift stores. Roberto wandered into a shop named "Sacred Gifts." The Mother Marys' had their own section. There was a separate Jesus section and an area for prominent saints. As he picked up pendants and effigies, old men and women, some priests and nuns, rifled through the piles. One lady, a nun, who looked vaguely familiar, turned over the objects rapidly, emphatically whispering "NO" each time. Although the objects were cheaply made, they sparkled. Among the heap of fakes, a precious pendant lay nestled in the bottom, her actions seemed to suggest.

He mimicked the nun, rummaging through the bins. She smiled at him, shaking her head. Finally, she picked up an oval locket adorned with an image of Mary clasping her hands in prayer. She held this one up to her face and kissed it. She began reciting the Hail Mary in Italian.

Then she began to tear.

He walked over to her.

She reached out her hands to hold his.

"It's okay," she said in broken English with an Italian accent.

"Did something happen?" he asked. "Can I help?"

"I'm fine, little Roberto," she said. "It's just that you don't remember me."

Now he was hit like a thunderbolt from the past. This was Sister Alberti from St. Patrick's.

As his face turned red, he held her hands tighter. He was flooded with fond memories of Sister Alberti. The classroom with the small wooden chairs and little desks bolted to them. The green, white and yellow uniforms, like the colors of Scotch tape. The twisted black face of the Jesus on the crucifix that hung in the center of the classroom. Sister Alberti's pink cheeks and bright, blue eyes. She'd aged so much in the past forty years. He recalled the questions he asked her in science class. Questions about the universe, about creation, about God. She was so patient.

"Yes, of course I remember you, Sister Alberti." They now embraced.

"Did you find what you were looking for in Lourdes?" she asked, her eyes wide and moist.

"I'm not sure what you mean, Sister," he said.

"What I mean to say is that now you must believe in miracles," she said.

"Was meeting you a miracle?" he asked.

"You still can't see what's right in front of you, little Roberto," she said. She handed him the oval locket adorned with an image of the Holy Mary she had picked up. It was a perfect replica of the statue that greeted him every morning in front of the entrance to St. Patrick's School so many years ago.

Slow Time

He is crouching on the grass behind a bush, out of wind. Only a few feet away he hears the growling of a tiger. He holds his breath until his lungs almost burst, cautiously letting the air seep out of his lungs.

The tiger lingers, but then seems to stroll away.

It doesn't matter what we call this being. He is half-man, half-beast. He speaks in a language of mixed grunts and gestures. His eye ridges are prominent. His teeth are crooked like planks of wood jammed into the earth. He looks like people we know, people that we've seen.

The coast now clear, he lifts his broad nose into the air to detect the scent of the tiger. Tigers are known to lay in wait, hiding from a distance so they can pounce on their unsuspecting victims, clawing the face, plunging their fangs into the neck and burrowing into the meat. Once the neck is penetrated, the body goes limp. The tiger knows that the moment the breath escapes the body, the flesh becomes tender and sweet.

The half-man remains still. He waits.

From this position he can see the light of the sun. He doesn't know what the sun is, but it's there every day, warming him. The sun feels good. He knows that when the sun is up, he can see better; he is less likely to step into the path of a predator. He squints looking up at the sun. The yellow colors wash over his face, as if caressing him. The sun doesn't talk to him; its hands touch him; its fingers massage his face. When the sun beats down on the grass, it's like it is laughing or dancing. His thinking about the sun is like what we think about at night when we can't sleep. You mull over images and ideas in your mind until they run into each other. You have wild, disconnected dream sequences that link thoughts which have occurred throughout the day, but all your thoughts are looped. They all lead to nowhere, a merry-go-round of imaginings. The half-man envisages a story: sitting by a river feeling the sun on his face, eating a gopher that he's hunted. The sun, the yellow, warmth, tiger, bush, sun, sky, yellow, the taste of meat. The yellow heat of the sun, the warmth. The sun's caress.

His thoughts drift away after a few moments. He lowers his head and closes his eyes. He dozes for a bit, waiting until the sun sets.

The sky is dark now. The moon, the sun's sister, comes out at night, staring over the land, casting a silver shadow.

It is safe to leave now.

He gets up quickly and runs. The night feels good. He dashes in the gray glow of the moon. You could not see your way in the darkness as he does. There are no signposts or directions. He just knows where he's going. It can't be described.

He'll have to stop soon. He must eat. Running for another few miles, he finds a creek, knowing that where there's water and food.

He hurriedly brushes through the shrubbery, looking for something edible; a bug, a flower or berries. He sees a brightly-colored, blue pansy. Pulling it out of the ground, he sniffs it, pleased by its perfumed fragrance. He expertly removes the pistils and stamens, throwing them to the ground, and stuffs the delicious petals into his mouth with his index finger. He then snatches up a worm that slinks along a leaf, stuffing it into his mouth. The worm tastes warm and wet. He eats berries from the bush and some leaves as well.

He then ambles down the little knoll to the creek. Looking right and left, he ladles cool water into his palm, quietly slurping it into his mouth. Squatting down in the grass, he shits and pees. It feels good.

He finds a place to sleep for an hour to replenish his energy. He clears a space, moving brushwood and small rocks out of the way. He lies down. At first, he is jittery, anxiously poking his head up and searching his surroundings. Then he hears the rustling of twigs on the ground. What is it? He waits. His eyes pierce the darkness, needing only the faint light of the shiny moon to see. He doesn't pick up an animal scent. He is still for a while. He determines there is nothing to be concerned about.

Then he puts his head down again, now lulled by the symphony of crickets. A coolness washes over his face. The night seeps into his skin. He drinks in the soft darkness. A gentle rain makes the air fresh and light.

He remembers earlier in the day how he bathed, like a lustful faun, in the warmth of the fair sun.

He soon falls asleep.

The Unending

We had recently moved into an apartment only a block away from an elevated train track. At times, the trains roared loudly, as if surging through our living room. Sometimes the train's rattle was subtle, like a gurgling brook. Sometimes we didn't hear the train at all.

One night, a few weeks ago, I got home very late from work. All of the lights were out in the apartment. On the kitchen table, I saw a cigarette still smoking in an ash tray, though I didn't see Triny, my wife. I figured she must have just gone to bed. I undressed, closed the lights and settled into bed.

But I couldn't sleep. The quiet made me nervous. I flopped on my stomach, then turned over on my back, unable to get comfortable. All I could hear was the screeching sounds of the trains pulling in and out of the station. My nerves jerked my body out of bed. I walked over to the bedroom window; the street was soundless and empty. Not a soul outside. I gazed out at the dark street.

I went to the kitchen to get the clearest view of the elevated train truss. Although slightly hidden by trees and shrubbery, I beheld the shadowy outline of a hulking train as it thundered by. I knew there'd be another train in a few minutes. I don't know what possessed me, but I quickly got dressed and put my sneakers on. Then I kissed Triny on the head lightly, so as not to wake her, and ran out into the dark night. Her hair felt cool and soft on my lips.

I was still tucking my heel into my sneaker as I ran to the station. Out of breath, the train lights flickered, now only just another stop away. Then, as the train pulled into the stop, its silver exterior sparkled in the station lights. Water poured from the top of the train, spilling down the sides. It must have just rained.

When the train doors opened, I stepped in. I had to cover my eyes to adjust to the flood of the brilliant light that washed over me. There were people sleeping with their mouths open, their heads leaning to one side.

I watched my apartment building drift away as the train took off. I wondered if Triny would notice I was gone. I hoped that she wouldn't worry.

I sat down next to a tall, thin man who held a book wide open in front of him. The book's title read 'The Ancient Curves.'

The man put the book down for a minute and looked at me.

"Do you know what time it is?" he asked. His eyes were watery and gray. As he spoke, strings of saliva webbed his mouth.

"I don't know," I said.

"Where are you headed?" he asked this time.

"I'm not exactly sure," I responded.

"This book explains how time works," said the man, pointing to 'The Ancient Curves.'

I nodded, wanting to hear more.

"You see," he now opened a page of the book. "This section refers to the great parabolas which traverse times and places." He pointed to an intricate picture that showed an entanglement of snakes, wrapped around each other, their heads facing different directions." The image was immensely detailed with incredibly fine curves and lines. I couldn't imagine how anyone could have drawn anything so tiny. The deeper I inspected the images, the more intricate the designs became. I then noticed the designs were moving, curling and weaving inside each other, like the living roots of a vast forest floor.

Gazing intently at the book, the man suddenly slammed it shut in one clapping motion, making a booming sound, like the closing of a castle door.

"So sorry, so sorry," he said. "I must be going; the book is yours now." He left the book on the seat. The train stopped suddenly; he exited as soon as the doors swished open.

I picked the book up, caressing it, turning the pages, completely entranced by the pictures. From what I could tell, the illustrations depicted narratives of time travel, showing tunnels warping and twisting into each other. There were no words in 'The Ancient Curves,' except for the title of the book. Yet the book appeared to possess incredible knowledge of the cosmos.

Then the train came to a sudden stop, jolting me out of a trance. What stop was this? I peered out the window and now noticed that the train was no longer moving on the track. The train seemed now to be sitting atop a rafter, propelled by a quietly humming engine. I panicked. Examining what used to be the tracks, I observed a long waterway. I gripped onto the train seat, as if trying to hold myself from falling. But falling where? And into what?

Then the train lunged forward, floating with the current of the water.

As the train made its stops, people came on and off speaking in different languages. This wasn't like trains I had been on in big cities with populations from all over the world. It seemed more like I was visiting others in their native towns.

An old Chinese man, wearing a straw hat but no shoes, walked into the car with fishing gear. He took a seat on the

35

train, blinking rapidly, embracing his fishing equipment, checking the stops on the board. Next to him was a woman robed in a bright red-and-pink dress, wearing a thorny, elaborate beaded hat. I thought that maybe she was from Thailand. The entire train was now filled with people who seemed to come from everywhere.

Suddenly I saw that the river channel we had been on now ran into a wide body of water, like a sea or an ocean. Where was I going? And what was happening? How will I get back home? I felt oddly safe, however, and believed that I'd be able to return. I couldn't explain why.

Now feeling like I was travelling in a boat instead of a train, I looked out into the water's endless blue. I could tell it was always summer here. The sun brightly sparkled on the ocean surface. Small, white clouds etched against the sapphire sky. There were seagulls flying overhead. I could smell the salt from the brine. For a second, the world felt like it was on a tilt and that I might slide off of it into some unknown oblivion. For just a second, the water around me threatened to upend and pour over me, drowning me in its infinite, azure bosom.

Like when a plane flies so high, or you look from a mountain top, the world opened up, and I could see everywhere at once. I reached out and found myself lifting off into the sky. And, somehow, I was now moving – not swimming – in the air. I knew that this wasn't a dream. There were others swimming in the air, too, including the Thai woman and the Chinese fisherman. Like a school of fish, there were countless human bodies swimming. Some were breast stroking. Some were doggie paddling. I saw the tall, thin man who handed me the book, lying on his back leisurely stroking the water. Where had I left the book?

Seeing a large, grey boulder in the distance, protruding from the ocean, I swam towards it, the sun glinting in my eye.

I swam faster and faster. I was exploding with a joy that completely engulfed me. I wanted to scream with laughter. I could hardly catch my breath. I tapped into something here, something that was only made possible by revelations I'd read in 'The Ancient Curves.'

When I made it to the boulder, I climbed on top of it. I observed that one patch of the horizon exposed a portal that pointed back to my house. Unlike the summer blue of this world, the portal showed a slightly gray sky. As I peered into the portal, I found myself suddenly airborne. I was now glimpsing into the window of my apartment building. And there was Triny. She was up, feeling around the bed. She looked worried, perhaps wondering where I'd gone. Seeing her this way made my heart feel heavy. I had done this to her.

I must have lost concentration. I was no longer hovering outside my bedroom window. I was now transported to a muddied landscape. The sky was fish-belly white. There were snarling dogs prowling the grounds and showing their fangs. A sudden glare from the moon made the landscape visible. I saw dog turds, torn clothing and clumps of hair. I almost stepped on a chewed-up human skull. It must have been in a place where a terrible battle had taken place. I observed a small-blue haze, a window to another world, and escaped as fast as I could.

Once again in the blue mist world, I spotted the grey vapor tunnel again. Triny was calling out my name. Her arms were outstretched towards the sky. She was crying. My heart felt heavy and saddened. I had to get to her. I reached into the gray mist, my hands piercing the slimy liquid sphere in which she was bounded. I was able to reach Triny's hands; they were on fire with warmth. We held wrists tightly. I wouldn't let go, even though my arms felt like they were going to fall off. I pulled as hard as I could, as if holding onto the reins of a train of powerful horses.

Wrenching her out, I then found myself flung on the floor, on my backside, my palms turned backwards. Triny was across from me – in the flesh.

"How did you find me?" I asked.

"I saw a blue haze just outside the bedroom window," said Triny, her jade-colored eyes bright and wide open. She was smiling.

"That's funny because I found my way to you because of the gray mist," I said. "I was so worried that you might have thought I had sleepwalked into a bus."

"My god, no," said Triny. "I just didn't know where you were. I was missing you." She paused then added, "I thought you didn't come home, that maybe you went home with someone else. I don't know." She started to cry.

"You couldn't be more wrong," I said, holding her hands in mine. "You know that I can't live without you. I need you." I stood up and reached out to help her up.

"I don't know what I'd do without you," said Triny. We held each other closely, like we might fall off of the earth itself if we didn't.

Then Triny silently pointed to the patch of blue sky above the trees. A pair of chirping magpies flew past us and landed atop one of the branches. As I turned to look, I saw a rainbow bridge arching across the sky. Leaning together to see the rainbow, Triny and I edged closer. I felt the heat of her cheek graze mine, our bodies now pressing against each other. Our lips touched. We held hands and started kissing. Almost on queue the sounds of birds peeping filled the air. The rainbow then disappeared, and the sky turned slightly less bright.

Eventually, we found our way back to the boat. The boat wended its way across rivers and bodies of water until it became a train. Then we were home again.

Now when I hear a train rumbling outside my window, I imagine the gurgling of a brook or the swirling of birds in the sky. I see frogs chasing insects. I see the broken bits of tree branches and leaves floating on the water. I feel the ocean that surrounds us all. And, with me always, is Triny. We're holding each other tightly like the world depends on us.

Everybody's Perfect, Nobody's Human

A live rock band pounds the walls of the arena. I had hardly woken up yet, my eyes nearly sealed shut from sleep. Only 9 a.m., a screeching guitar scrapes the soft tissue of my brain like a ragged saw, clawing at my hangover.

After a blaring keynote speech, there is a thirty-minute break. My boss, Hermann, and I try to find a quiet spot to do my quarterly review. The band never takes a break, so we shout over the clanging music, discussing my end of year performance.

"Quite a show this year, eh?" he asks, pointing to the stage behind him, his smile wrinkling the tight skin on his boney face. His bald head is like a pirate skull, small eyes sunk deep in its remote caverns.

"I can't believe the magnitude of the whole thing," I say, feigning my scorn. I hardly like going to rock concerts, much less attending weeklong corporate putsches.

"I mean, twenty-thousand people in a stadium singing 'We Are the Champions' is impressive," I say. My face turns a swollen red from swallowing the truth. My entire being quivering beneath the skin.

Hermann's gaze lingers for a moment. He sniffs the air, like he smells the stink of my fib.

"Reviewing your year," Hermann exhales, now turning to his laptop, "you only obtained 95% of your quota." The bones of his baldpate push up against his cranium like they're about to explode.

"You know that you need to achieve 125% of quota?" he says. Now his eyeballs roll up into their sockets, escaping view, like a turtle's head sucking up into its shell.

"Work will set you free," he continues, now repeating Dr. Gerry.

Yesterday, Dr. Gerry lectured the entire company in an arena, offering advice on how to achieve heroic work feats, inspiring us to become the next Steve Jobs. All, of course, in the name of the company's profits. He didn't provide instruction on how to battle struggled sleep and manage your increasing consumption of alcohol.

Alcohol ran from every spigot, every night at every event. You needed to pour a river of anesthesia into your veins to withstand the freight train that ran into you every day. And to help you forget so you can do it again the next day and the next.

Dr. Gerry evangelized about how we needed to use meditation to remain grounded in the eye of the storm.

"I came from a poor family," said Dr. Gerry, as twenty-thousand people sat gripped by his speech.

"My father was an alcoholic." He paused and took a deep breath. Silence swept over the amphitheater.

Dr. Gerry was young and handsome, like a movie star. As he spoke, the screen behind him flashed pictures of him posing with famous athletes, heads of state and executives of the company. He talked about how he'd chosen this path to help people and ultimately write his best-seller "Everybody's Perfect, Nobody's Human."

"I learned to discover my perfection in his imperfection," he added. "Watching my father crumble, falling down in the street, brought home, face bloodied, by the cops," he paused, now crying. "I made every day a lab experiment in my goal to reach perfection." Wiping the tears from his face, he added, "I worked two jobs, one in the morning and one at night, and went to college classes in between."

In the stunning stillness, you could hear people swallowing the lumps in their throats. "After my mother died of cancer, I raised my two little brothers while completing my PhD at Harvard."

He concluded by chanting "work will set you free," until the entire arena chanted along with him. Then he brought his hands together in prayer and bowed.

"Did you hear what I said?" asks Hermann, snapping me out of my dream. I had been lost in Dr. Gerry's speech from yesterday.

"I don't want to make excuses," I say, knowing none would suffice. Why wasn't I willing to stab myself in the eye and bleed to death for the company? Why wasn't I able to give my all, like Matteo? Matteo hasn't been home in weeks, Hermann had once said. He hasn't seen his kids or his wife in a month. And he's able to fly around the country to meetings despite his recent heart attack.

"Don't you want to be on stage next year in the Ring of Perfection?" asks Hermann.

Standing in the Ring of Perfection meant that you had outperformed in every metric. You received a large cash bonus, stock options and a trip to the French Riviera. In the center of the ring, high above the people, was a great flame, flapping and twisting. I wondered how people didn't feel the heat from the flame. The flame roared higher and higher, lapping at times, out of control. It looked like it could burn the whole stadium down.

I imagined jumping into the flame. If I can't be in the Ring of Perfection, maybe I could just die a perfect death in its bosom. What mattered anymore now? I felt numb from the deafening repetition of work, from the emptiness of failure.

Scanning the plates of eggs scattered about the tables, I envy my peers. They can eat eggs like this with gluttony, spooning the runny, synthetic goop into their mouths with insect like voracity. I am resentful of their ravenous appetites and iron stomachs. Eating one morsel of that inedible junk made my insides twist, as if I had jammed sandpaper into the knotted bundle of my intestines.

WORK WILL SET YOU FREE.

"You know we're going to have our status meeting every week," Hermann says. "It's not going to change. I need you to demonstrate progress," he adds, taking a drink of water. I'm wondering if this is difficult for him, too.

"As of right now, I can't see you making it through the year."

"You know I'm working hard."

"You have to work harder."

"I did almost hit my quota," I say.

"Look, there is no why here," he replies, hearing the tone in my voice. "We will check in next week, the week after that and the week after that. There are two outcomes. You bring in the numbers, or you're out." There's no venom in his voice.

"We have an opportunity here to pull ahead of the pack. Everyone needs to pull their weight."

I am silent, thinking about how all year long we heard that our numbers were flagging; each region was slack, and heads were going to roll. And yet, at the convention, we celebrated record growth. Our company was so rich we bought another company for billions of dollars – without, as yet, a clear purpose.

The band starts playing "We Are the Champions" again for the third time this morning.

Hermann suddenly rises from his seat, stretching his arms out, stomping his feet and now singing "And I never lose," along with Queen.

I feel a tingling from my spine as I stare, bewildered, at Hermann. A sinister chill tickles my body, like a snake has entered through my toe, arresting my entire being, escaping from my mouth.

Spitting and coughing uncontrollably, I am thrust to the ground, as if by a devil.

Hermann bends over, putting his hand on my shoulder, thinking perhaps that he's given me a heart attack. I reach out for his hand and pull myself up. A warm puddle of vomit is just behind my throat. I can taste it on my tongue.

Finally, I'm standing like a man in the drunk tank with Hermann. I am thirsty. I am suffocating. I need something, but I don't know what.

Hermann's look of despair is encouraging. Unable to hold it back any long, I throw up on his shirt.

He doesn't even look at the puke now oozing onto the ground from his shirt.

I gaze into his eyes with appreciation.

This is the most human moment I've felt in days.

The Purest Rain

I once was, we once were, ordinary people, like you. Being together we have become one mind.

I am sorry if our writing is clumsy; we don't speak, write or use words any longer. Our thoughts are felt by each other before we have them. The ideas of I and we aren't as clear as they may be for you, our ancestors. We are all we; we are all I. I am writing it to you as if we were I so that my message can be understood. We have been sending our message to you in the form of rain, wind and dreams. We understand that you can't hear us. So, we write this letter of love to you. We hope you will read it.

When we left the earth, our crew was young. We were sent in the wild hope of finding another hospitable world.

The earth's climate spiraled into instability. The polar ice caps melted to unrecoverable levels, making the oceans pour onto the coasts, crushing cities, engulfing countless lives. There were hurricanes and storms. The skies had become hellfire.

I volunteered. What was left for me? Our precious world was on the verge of collapse. I never felt that I belonged anyway. I vaguely recall the person who I was, a young scientist and a restless seeker. I was a loner, awkward, incapable of having relationships. I was more content in the computer lab than in the company of people. I had hoped to escape the earth, to go as far

47

away from humanity as possible, I didn't realize I'd be heading smack into the center of humanity itself.

We left our families, our friends and lives on the green-blue planet. We were hurled out into space, tossed like a message in a bottle.

The moment we launched into space, I felt even my name slipping away. Seeing the earth transform into a distant dot was like watching my own mind vanish. It saddened me to think that everything I'd ever known, every place I'd ever been, would be gone forever. And though I had a pang in my stomach, I also felt exhilarated. Everything would be out there now, beyond this world.

Given the immense distances of intergalactic travel, we had to find ways to extend our lives. It was a matter of life or death. Being a crew of scientists, every moment was spent in our test labs, experimenting and discovering. First, we began implanting synthetic parts in our bodies. The artificial implants slowly took over our organs and other functions. By the time we left our solar system, the average age of our crew was one hundred and fifty. Those who had lived, lived because they endured genetic modifications, complete replacements of hearts, brains, eyes and bodies. Those whose implants or genetic modifications weren't successful, died.

When we reached the outer spiral of the Milky Way, our entire crew was remade in our manufactured image. Not a fleshy eyeball among us. Two hundred and fifty years had passed. Communications with Earth became intermittent, our replies lapsing over decades. The further we travelled, the more distant the memories became, the less distinct we became to each other. There were now only one hundred or so of us. Being together in a capsule floating in space, far away from civilization, forced us to become intimately close. And, as the centuries passed, our interactions transcended conversation.

Being together became *together being*. I remember being at a music concert or a sports event when I was on Earth. Everyone connected in a single emotion. The roar of many like one. This is like *together being*.

After travelling more than four hundred light-years, the earth then only a memory, like an ancient myth of our past, we began to shuck off our genetically modified bodies. Our minds, like vines in a peaty moss, wound and tangled into each other. Where did one mind end and another begin? Imagine never being alone, never feeling completely empty. All our emotions touched. Where someone had previously felt alone or frightened, the others anticipated these feelings and rushed to them. The speed of thoughts and feelings reached a rapid pace. Conversations between people were heard by everyone. Knowledge that one person may have held in their own head became shared. Learning became learning for everyone. Our bodies remained but were vacated. Our minds, like wind, swarmed into each other. Things like shame disappeared. When everyone's ideas were exposed and felt by each other, it no longer mattered how private they were.

At some point, even our spaceship slipped off us like a nightgown. We didn't need it any longer. We travelled in unison, beyond light speed in something we call forever now. We are everywhere at all times.

In fact, we are with you now. We are like invisible ghosts swarming around you. We live your sadness and fears. And joys. We are whispering to you, hoping someday you'll hear us. We want to take you into our bosom. We want to shower you in our tears until we are all joined in one gentle downpour of the purest rain.

All of The Days

"I'm taking Miles to the hospital now," my wife Martha said, her voice shaky.

"Is it a stomach virus?" I asked.

"The doctor said that it's possibly appendicitis," she answered.

Earlier that day, when he first woke up, our six-year-old, Miles, was holding his stomach in pain and then threw up violently. But in an hour or so, before I left the house for work, he was lying on the couch playing video games. He seemed okay. But later, he started pointing to a specific place where the pain hurt most. That's when Martha took him to the doctor.

"I'm going to leave the office in a bit," I replied, while writing a note on my computer. I wasn't completely sure what appendicitis was, but I didn't think it was serious anyway.

"My son's doctor says he might have appendicitis," I said to a colleague at work, after I hung up with Martha.

"Has it burst? The appendix?" he asked.

"I don't know," I said.

At first, he didn't say anything, but then suddenly blurted, "Appendicitis can be serious." Then he whispered, "If it isn't caught in time, it could be fatal."

I called Martha back immediately, trying to stay calm. "I'm leaving the office now," I said. I then left everything and ran for the door.

By some miracle, I rushed into the emergency room just in time to find Martha walking in the midst of a team of doctors, pushing Miles on a gurney into a triage room. Due to the utter improbability of this happening, I expected to see angels flanking the gurney.

The rest of the evening felt like it was speeding furiously down an icy slope.

Moaning and holding his stomach, Miles asked for a drink of water. The nurse said I couldn't give him water. "Can I wet his lips with a sponge?" I asked. Miles' lips were parched. His eyes were wet with fear. His wild, curly, blond hair splayed out on the bed, piling up behind his head like billowing clouds. His little palms were outstretched as he leaned back.

The nurse handed me a sponge on a stick; it looked like a Popsicle. I rubbed it over Miles' lips and tongue to moisten them. I had wetted my father's lips like this when he was dying of cancer in the hospital twenty-five years prior.

Various doctors streamed in and out of the triage room, introducing themselves and shaking our hands. I didn't want to meet or talk to anyone.

We were then told that Miles would have to be hurried into surgery in an hour or so. Now rushed to another room, we met Doctor Lawrence, the main physician overseeing Miles. While my head was spinning, Doctor Lawrence spoke clearly and slowly, his large, white teeth strong and bony like ivory tusks.

"His appendix has burst. We're going to remove his appendix and clean out the area around it, you see, making sure it's not infected," the doctor said. His shirt was meticulously tucked in, his slacks perfectly ironed. Doctor Lawrence spoke from a place of absolute calm as my mind swirled. While the skies of my mind raged and thundered, he was unaffected and composed.

Did he say the appendix burst? I asked him a few questions: "Will this be laparoscopic surgery? How long will recovery take?" My thoughts were scrambled. I spoke as if under water, like my words floated across the room, drowned and muted. Doctor Lawrence gave me clear and precise answers. I found myself absent-mindedly focused on the smoothness of his skin and the delicate wrinkles around his eyes. I marveled at how well he was aging. I estimated that he was in his late 50s, only a few years older than me. I was somewhere between trusting Doctor Lawrence and wanting to be like him.

"What's going to happen?" Miles asked. I explained that the doctor would have to take out his appendix. "Will it hurt?" he asked.

"You'll be asleep. You won't feel a thing," I reassured him. I held his hand and stroked his hair. Miles asked if he could wear a surgical cap, like the doctors and his assistants wore. I said that we would get him a cap. For the first time, he started to whimper.

"I want a cap," he demanded, now starting to cry. "I want a cap." He'd been so brave and calm; he was getting panicked. The distress had crept up on him, like a spider. The word surgery was ominous, even to a six-year-old.

One of the assistants handed me a cap, and I wrapped it around Miles' head, tucking the soft, blond curls inside. He looked like a saint with a golden halo. Then his terror somewhat subsided. I could see tomorrow through his windowed eyes. I saw skies and oceans. Something miraculous was happening, like he had one foot in infinity.

Then the doctors rolled his gurney away to the operating room, leaving us behind, our hands extended, as if they dropped him away on a slalom course, disappearing down the mountain.

He was out of our control. Martha and I turned toward each other without speaking. We held each other, took turns sighing. Neither of us cried. I felt like running out onto the highway smack into a truck. My mind was trapped in a tumbler, as thoughts, emotions and objects smashed into each other, like clothes in a dryer, rolling and tossing, rolling and tossing.

We took a walk outside to get some air and settle our minds. The sky was large and indifferent above us, curled around the gray clouds like a black beast. My mind was folding in on itself, collapsing into a murky hole that grew smaller and smaller. Martha and I held hands and hugged. Our job was to keep it together.

When we returned, the nurse at the desk directed us to an empty waiting room. "This is it?" I asked. It was the size of a large closet.

"He's claustrophobic," explained Martha.

The nurse shrugged her shoulders. "The doctor will come get you when the operation is over," she said. I squirreled into my seat and put my feet up on another chair. While Martha ate Reese's Pieces and donuts, I had a few stale Budweisers, since that's all they had at the bodega we stopped in on our walk. After what seemed like many long hours, Doctor Lawrence appeared in the waiting room. He was still wearing his surgery cap. "Everything went well," he said, smiling. I couldn't help noticing his perfect white elephant tusk teeth again. His voice was very reassuring. As he spoke, his eyes settled on the can of Budweiser. I felt reckless and savage.

After talking for a few minutes, shaking hands, not really understanding all of the details, I got the general notion that the surgery went well, and that Miles was okay. Miles would be sore, but he was expected to recover in a few days.

Doctor Lawrence reached out and handed me his card. "I want you to call me, after he's out of the hospital. I'd like to share some new therapies, new ideas with you."

The days that followed were a mixture of joy that Miles was all right and the worry that we had caught it just in time. We had all become closer as a result of the trauma. He was then released from the hospital after five days. He started sleeping in our bed as soon as we brought him home. We all needed to be together. Miles seemed to age a year or two in those few days.

Weeks later, I called Doctor Lawrence to make an appointment, as he had requested. The receptionist said that Martha and I should come alone, without Miles.

"So good to see you," said Doctor Lawrence when we arrived, his white teeth baring their recognizable shine. We all exchanged handshakes. "And how is Miles?"

"He's doing well," replied Martha, "thanks to you."

He pointed to the chairs for us to sit. "I'm so glad you're both here," he said, pulling out two folders with materials in them. He placed the folders on his desk. "Now, I'm going to need you to sign these confidentiality papers. They're concerning some profound new research that will be of interest regarding your son. But I can't talk about it until you sign first." He pushed the folders toward us.

We both sat back in our chairs. "Is this concerning Miles's health?" asked Martha.

"Yes, it is," Doctor Lawrence answered. We then both reached across the desk and signed the documents. We had no idea of what was to come next.

"You see, I've been doing studies on children, especially on aging," he continued, his voice suddenly sounding deeper, more serious. "I've made some very interesting progress in my research, frankly. Discoveries that will radically change the world forever." This didn't sound like the humble doctor we'd met at the hospital. What could he be talking about? And why invite us here to tell us? He went on, "You see, with our work in genetics, coupled with new findings in cellular regeneration, we've made some significant advances in what makes the body grow and, more importantly, age."

I remained silent. I felt deferential to the man, even though I wasn't sure what he was talking about. After all, he did just effectively save our son's life. But Martha, I could tell, was annoyed, shifting around in her seat. She winced and shook her head. "Excuse me, doctor, but why are you telling us this?" she suddenly blurted out. "I mean, especially after all we've been through." He stopped speaking and looked at us over the rim of his glasses. "Please excuse me," continued Martha. "I don't mean to be rude, but," she paused and looked at me now, still speaking to Doctor Lawrence, "are you trying to sell us something? Do you have special vitamins or shots? What's this about, really?"

"Now, now, I do understand," apologized Doctor Lawrence. His eyes looked sorrowful as he scratched his head. "This is all a lot to talk about, I agree. Maybe we should just do this another time."

"There'll be no other time," said Martha curtly. "I'm paying a babysitter, I've worked all day, and, if you don't mind, I'd rather that we not waste each other's time." A deafening silence followed, like a blanketed quiet after a loud car crash. She began to get up, so I stood up, too.

"It's just that, well, I wanted to offer something to you, your husband and Miles," he said.

"Okay," said Martha. "Say it now, or I'm walking out the door."

Doctor Lawrence folded his arms across his chest and sat back. "You see, we've developed methods that can allow a child to, well, remain a child forever." He handed us pictures of other children. Martha and I looked at the photos, passing them back and forth. He said, "I know, it sounds absurd. These children are twenty-six years old. They've been in our program for twenty years." They each looked to be about six years old.

"Look at this," he said, and then flashed up a video from his computer onto the wall. The video showed a twenty-year stretch of a child and his parents. The voiceover narration explained that the parents in the film had their child later in life. The film condensed the passage of twenty-years into a few minutes. In one scene, the child was stroking the thin, gray hair of his now old father lying sick in a hospital bed.

Martha held her hand to her throat like she was losing breath. I put my arm on her shoulder, thinking that she'd lunge at Doctor Lawrence. "My research has shown that we can suspend the growth process and consequently slow aging to a crawl," he said serenely.

Finally gathering up the courage to speak, I asked, "But what does this all mean and why us?"

"That's a very good question," said Doctor Lawrence. "The truth is, first of all, I really like you both, and I really like Miles. There was something in your patience and calm that was inspiring to me." He paused. "No doubt," he added, "Miles reminds me of my son, who's now in his late twenties. His manner, his quiet wisdom. Even his curly, blond hair. His innocence." He looked down at his desk. "Even doctors are people, after all," he added.

"Why didn't you put your own son in the program?" I asked.

"Researchers aren't allowed to recommend family members," said Doctor Lawrence.

"Are you saying he'd permanently stay six years old?" I continued.

"Yes, he wouldn't grow old, he wouldn't get sick. He'd remain a six-year-old for a few hundred years."

A few hundred years.

"We'd be robbing him of his life," said Martha.

"You'd be giving him more life. You'd be expanding his life." the doctor replied.

"But he wouldn't go to his high school prom, or go to college or go on a date?" Martha asked.

"No, he would stay the same perfect little boy that he is now. Don't you think you'll miss holding his little hand in yours, taking care of him, putting him to sleep?"

"This is ridiculous," I huffed. "We thank you for your time..." I started to say.

"But we'd have our sweet little boy to hold in our arms until we're old people," said Martha, her voice softening now. "We could read stories every night to put him to sleep, even when we're old. He would wear the same little shoes, ride his little bike forever." She looked at the wall when she spoke, like she was talking to an invisible person. "He would never lose that sweet little voice," she said, tears now streaming down her face. Doctor Lawrence nodded his head in agreement.

"Wait, wait, wait," I said. "While this is all very fascinating, I have to say that I'm very uncomfortable with all of this."

"Of course, of course," said Doctor Lawrence. "This is an unbelievable and difficult thing for anyone. We've been working with a very select group of parents. The first reaction is shock."

Now I was the one trying to leave. I reached out for Martha's hand and pulled her up out of her chair. She wiped the wetness from her face. "Let's go home and talk about this. Let's think for a few days, maybe a few weeks, maybe more," I said. "I just don't know."

Shaking our hands, Doctor Lawrence agreed wholeheart-edly, walking us to the door. "Take your time, think it over," he said. Opening the door for us, he added, "Please remember that this is confidential."

As we walked out into the night air, I wanted to break away, running as fast as I could. Martha and I were silent the entire drive home.

The Three Bridges

Overlooking the Naples River, Maria Tuttolomundo's apartment has a perfect view of the Three Bridges. On a clear day, the light from the Three Bridges sparkles off the Naples River. The Nina Bridge, the largest of the three, materializes out of the left side of her bay window, and the two sister bridges, the Pinta and the Santa Maria, emerge out of the right side. There is no other collection of bridges like this in North America. Maria often looks out her window, daydreaming. Sometimes she curls up in the kitchen nook by the window to have morning coffee. And at night, she'll sit on her couch to gaze out the window at the Three Bridges. Maria feels lucky to have lived in this apartment since completing her PhD in Astrophysics three years ago.

One day, leaving for work in a rush, Maria dashes out of her apartment, bumping into a man walking down the street.

"Excuse me," she says, her padded shoulder now lodged in his neck. The man is clearly shocked. Blinking, flustered from the suddenness of their collision, he places his hands on her shoulders as if to get a good look as his assailant.

"Are you okay?" she asks.

"It's fine. I'm fine," he replies, rubbing his eyes as if to wake himself up. He speaks with an accent.

"I'm so sorry."

They lock eyes for more than a second. They are almost the same height, maybe near the same age.

"I live right here," says Maria, pointing to the window above the door to her apartment. There is a vase with red and pink flowers sitting on the ledge.

Now smiling, the man says, "And I live only a few blocks away. Imagine."

"Nice to meet you," says Maria, now shaking his hand. "But I have to go," she adds.

Maria reaches into her purse and pulls out a business card.

"I'm a good neighbor; let me make it up to you," she says. "Call me."

The man rolls the card over with his thumb and index finger, nodding approval.

"And nice to meet you too, Doctor Tuttolomundo," he says, emphasizing the word 'doctor' as she pulls away.

"I am Vito Mangavacallo," he shouts into his right hand held up to his face. She waves walking away, heading towards a bus across the street.

For a moment, he worries that she'll get hit by an oncoming car. In a few seconds, she is swallowed into the bus and whisked away with the morning traffic.

A few days later, Vito calls Maria. They talk for a bit and arrange a get-together in their neighborhood for a drink.

When they meet at the Vesuvius Bar on Main Street, Maria is already sitting on a stool. She's drinking a martini.

They shake hands.

"One for me too, please," he says to the bartender, pointing at her drink.

"So how long have you lived in this neighborhood?" asks Vito, settling into his chair.

"For three years, since I finished school."

"Oh yes, you must tell me about that. You are a doctor, yes?"

"Yes, I went to school in California to study astrophysics. I'm a research scientist."

"Very impressive," says Vito.

"And you?"

"Well, I am a scientist of sorts," replies Vito.

For the first time, Maria notices the sculpted curvature of his face. He's handsome. His eyes are a soft, bright green. *And he knows how to dress*, she thinks to herself.

"In fact, I am a magician."

"A what?" Maria asks, slightly laughing to herself.

"No, really. I do events, shows. I make a good living from it." He pauses. "You mean you haven't heard of me?"

She shakes her head no; then they both laugh.

"Where did you learn how to do magic?"

"Back in Italy. In Venice. I studied with Silvan, the Illusionist, as he is known, after completing my degree in Chemistry at the University of Bologna."

"Why did you study magic?"

"Magic is just another branch of science," replies Vito. "As a student of Silvan, I began my scientific study of the paranormal."

"There is a scientific study of the paranormal?" she asks, taking a sip of her martini.

"In fact, there are institutions devoted to the study. You even have them in America. At Duke University. We study telepathy, precognition, telekinesis and clairvoyance."

"That's fascinating," says Maria, stating it almost as a question, trying to suppress the surprise in her voice.

"So, you are a scientist," she says, forcing a sigh of relief.

'Of course, I am a scientist on the fringe," he says, now chuckling.

Maria laughs with him. *Maybe this paranormal thing isn't so terrible*, she thinks.

They raise their glasses to toast.

"Here's to feeling like I've met you before," says Vito.

"Yes, you do seem very familiar," she replies.

They clink glasses.

After a few drinks, their conversation engaging and relaxed, Maria considers whether to invite him to her place. *Like some men, he's not competing with me*, she thinks. *He's funny and kind. And smart.*

"Would you like to take a walk?" asks Vito. "It's a beautiful night."

"Yes, that would be nice."

After they exit the Vesuvius, they walk around the block, heading unintentionally towards Maria's apartment.

There is a slight chill in the air. The moon shines above them, casting a soft, silver shadow on the street.

Since they are near her apartment, Maria now works up the courage to ask if Vito wants to come up and have a night cap.

"I have a view of the Three Bridges that's spectacular."

"The Three Bridges? I would love that."

Now in the apartment, sitting in the kitchen nook near the bay windows, they settle in, each holding a glass of wine in their hands.

"What made you want to study astrophysics?" asks Vito.

"I've always been interested in how things work. I've been especially curious about the cosmos. How stars are formed. The distances between stars. The age of galaxies."

Vito listens, watching her every movement as she speaks. Her lips are red and full. Her black hair rolls gently down her shoulders, like a soft rain. She's very pretty.

Interrupting herself, raising her hand, Maria offers to get one of the books she has written from the bookshelf in her bedroom. She's excited to share with him what she's been working on.

They get up together, almost bumping into each other.

She disappears into the back of the apartment.

Now Vito is strolling around her living room, looking at the paintings on the wall. They are lovely. There are two matching rectangular canvasses; they are brushed white with soft hues of light-amethyst colored swirls. The canvasses have a sandpaper surface. Vito reaches out to touch the surface of one of the paintings, rubbing his finger on the rocky granules. Oddly, the canvas seems to catch fire. It's as if there are flames shooting out of his hands. *What is this*, he thinks. *Am I doing a magic trick on myself?* He pats down the little flame that started. Now he walks over to the lamp nestled in the corner. It is made of paper. Without touching the lamp, it too is set aflame. "What is wrong with me," he says aloud, not knowing what is happening or what to do.

As he hears the patter of Maria's feet coming from the backroom, Vito smothers the lamp shade fire with his palms.

Now in the living room, book in hand, Maria sniffs the air.

"Something on fire?"

Vito is not sure what to say. He shrugs. He's not certain if anything really happened or if his mind is playing tricks on him. Maybe he's nervous. *This is too good to be true. There must be something wrong*, he thinks. *And if there isn't, perhaps my mind is trying to sabotage the night. She's too perfect for me. Too smart. Too pretty.*

They sit down together to examine the book. The title is 'Where Are They?'

He takes the book into his hands.

"Fermi's Paradox," he says, referring to Enrico Fermi's statement: If there is intelligent life in the universe, where is everybody?

"Vito, you know Fermi's Paradox?"

He likes hearing her say his name.

"Maria, my dear, first of all, I, too, am a scientist," he says, curling his fingers in his hands to accentuate his point.

"And I am Italian."

"Yes, yes, of course."

"There is an estimated 70 sextillion (7×1021) stars in the observable universe," he recites from memory, turning the pages of her book.

"And even if intelligent life occurs on only a tiny percentage of planets around these stars, it suggests that there's the possibility of life, of intelligent life," she completes his sentence, almost whispering the last word.

They are both stunned.

"And that's only the observable universe," says Maria. "What's beyond that which is observable?"

"There are more things in heaven and earth than are dreamt of in your philosophy," says Vito, quoting Shakespeare. They both laugh.

"That's what's exciting to me about all of this," says Maria. "It's the vastness of the universe. The fact that we go about living our lives, focusing on our small worlds when there is so much out there. So much we don't know. It boggles my mind."

"This is why I am a magician," says Vito.

"But you are a scientist, too."

"We only know what we know. There is still so much to discover. I find myself unable to be pinned down to studying only what we know. I need to be free to ask even scientific questions. I don't want to be boxed in."

Oh no, thinks Maria. *Is this when the speech comes about not being able to be committed to someone?* She's not even looking for a commitment. At least not yet. But the speech. The speech. The speech is more annoying than anything else.

"But you," continues Vito, "you have achieved great things. I could learn so much from someone as brilliant as you."

"That is very generous of you to say," she says, thankful he didn't wax the speech.

"I am more a philosopher of science, than a strict scientist. I need to ask the big questions, the questions that science, at least to date, can't answer."

"Like what?" asks Maria.

"Like why are we here? Are we an error in the fabric? Are there others like us?"

He is earnest. I like that. He's not a braggart, thinks Maria.

"We have the same goal," she says, pointing to her book title, 'Where Are They?'

"What if I told you that I dreamed about meeting you days before we met?" asks Vito.

"As a scientist, I would say that I don't have enough data to make any definitive statements on this. Maybe you saw me on the street." She doesn't say that she had dreamt about a handsome magician a few nights ago.

"But you agree, it does feel like we've met before?"

"I have to admit it does."

"It's uncanny, isn't it? After all we know, there is so much yet that is inexplicable."

"That's what drives my scientific curiosity," she says.

"And since we're at it, can you explain the smell of fire from before?" he asks.

"No, I wondered where that came from."

Neither of them pursues the conversation further.

Now Vito gently exhales, fixing the crease in his pants, then folds his hands together and places them on his thigh.

"Well, maybe that's enough for tonight, no?" says Vito. "I hope I haven't bored you to death."

"No, I am curious to know more about a philosopher of science. And I'd love to hear more about Venice, about Italy and your studies."

Suddenly, Vito realizes that Maria's hands are on his. Even she doesn't know how that happened. Now Maria and he are both silent, looking into each other's faces.

His hands are soft and warm, she thinks.

A thick stillness envelops the apartment, as if time has stopped.

In the next moment, anything can happen, they both think.

Vito wants to kiss her but doesn't want to ruin the moment. *Why risk defeat,* he thinks. *And, even worse, what if she kisses me back? Too much to consider. This night has been perfect. It would be best to end it now. We will have tomorrow and then the next day.*

"So, maybe I should get going, yes?" asks Vito.

"I have work to do anyway," says Maria. *Let this beautiful moment linger on,* she considers. *What's the rush?*

As he gathers his things up, he looks out the bay window.

"I've had a most lovely night."

"Me too."

"I think we should do something again. Soon," he adds.

"That would be wonderful."

"Maybe we can go to hear music. The opera."

"I love opera."

"Somehow I knew you did," says Vito, his eyes beaming with joy.

"You have my card."

"Yes, I'll call you, or you can call me," he says, giving her his card.

The card reads Dr. Mangavacallo.

She takes the card, and they embrace. They kiss each other on the cheek, then he leaves.

As she picks up the empty wine glasses, looking out at the view of the Three Bridges, she can't help but feel giddy. A magician philosopher? And a scientist, too?

Still smelling the burnt odor, she follows the source to one of the paintings. She leans into the painting and sniffs. It's hard to tell if the painting is burned or if it just looks like it's burned.

That's weird, she thinks to herself. She is reminded of the dream she had a few nights ago. It was indeed strange. The handsome magician in her dream had fingers that exploded with fire. Even in her dream she knew that fingers couldn't shoot fire from their tips. There had to be a scientific explanation. It had to be an illusion. A trick.

Now sitting in front of her bay window, her book in her hand, she looks out at the view of the Three Bridges feeling lucky.

The Long Way

After work, Philip stops at Parisi's bakery to buy a loaf of bread. He walks home from the office, same route every day, like he's done for the last forty years.

"Hello Rita," he says to the woman behind the counter. Rita is portly, her hair is piled in a bun on her head. She's about the same age as Philip.

Without even asking, Rita slides the seeded loaf into a long paper bag.

"No ham and cheese, please," says Philip, smiling.

"No, sir," says Rita, simpering; she knows the routine.

He tucks the loaf under his arm and ambles down the street, lazily waving his free arm.

Then Philip strolls into Vick's Hardware, wending his way to the electrical supply section. He picks up a voltage meter, turns it around and pushes up his glasses to read the label carefully. A newfangled electrical tester even? Maybe time to replace the old one.

"And look who it is" says Vick, emerging from the backroom, reaching out to shake Philip's hand.

"Just the man I'm looking for," says Philip. They begin discussing a new project that Philip is considering. He's thinking about installing new socket adapters in the apartment. Lots of projects, lots of things to do. Vick shows him various tools and equipment, the two of them discussing the pros and cons of each.

Leaving the store with a bag of electrical hardware, Philip then turns the corner to his apartment.

After dinner, Philip looks out the window of his kitchen. The street is lively. The sun shimmers on the trembling, green leaves. Children are playing ball in the apartment vestibule. A young father calls to his children to come eat dinner. The man is handsome, like Philip. He has straight black hair, long thin legs, wearing a suit with a vest.

That looks just like me, when I was twenty-five, thinks Philip. But I never wanted kids. To be honest, I never really liked kids.

Having studied electrical engineering, Philip was recruited by GL Engineering as a quality control manager straight out of college. He was immediately making money. By twenty-five, he bought an Alfa Romeo to tear down the highways, cigarette hanging out of the side of his mouth, feeling the wind blow through his hair. There was nothing he couldn't do.

The first years at GL Engineering were charged with fire. Philip had a purpose. His job was to ensure the quality of the machine parts that would be installed in airplanes. He often contemplated the importance of the work, how the planes flying overhead carried people safely to faraway places. He was proud that his work made it possible for families to go to Hawaii, or to the beaches in Miami, California. Sometimes he dreamed at night about airplanes flying at hundreds of miles an hour, zigzagging across the globe, flying over and around his bed. It was as if he was the center of activity, the beehive.

At work, he often ate alone; his mind would run over the steps he planned out. Sometimes he talked out loud to himself. But none were as good as Philip at testing the parts, running over the control methods, some of which he authored. Other people had families to go home to, things to do after work. Not

Philip. In the early years, he'd stay until the evening, calibrating, measuring and testing. Over and over again. As long as it took.

Then one day he met Sarah. She was a salesperson from one of the machine parts companies. He saw her through a glass divider in the office, holding a briefcase, taking notes as she talked to one of the product managers.

When they were introduced, she shook his hand firmly. He noticed her thick, red lipstick.

"Nice to finally meet you, Philip," she said. "You're a legend here at GL. It's like I know you already since I see your name on manuals and in reports," she added.

They now often talked on the phone. Philip admitted to himself that she knew her machine parts.

They reviewed inventory reports one time over lunch. They had a lot in common, both being from small towns, both being hard-working. She studied engineering, too. Soon they were dating. After a few months, Sarah wanted to know where things were going.

"I like you very much," she said.

"I like you, too," he replied.

They often talked around things. Even when they kissed, it was like their lips never touched. Or like their lips were very dry.

One day, Sarah said that they should be apart temporarily.

"I need time to think," she said, nearly crying. She couldn't even hold his hand when she spoke. They would be apart for now, only. For now, she repeated. So she could get her thoughts together.

Philip was disturbed in the manner of someone missing a train and who now had to wait on the platform, alone. It was inconvenient. Sarah's heart, meanwhile, bled.

A whole year went by before she saw him again at the office.

Philip was very cordial, almost too cordial. He talked about his work, about how his processes produced the finest working components. Sarah listened, knowing now he was too far away from everything to feel anything for her. Not the way she needed him to feel for her.

"I'll call you," he said when she walked away. On the other side of the door, she held her fist to her heart and cried.

Philip went to lunch.

That was all a long time ago. Forty years ago.

As if he merged into the gears of a clock, Philip slipped into a series of endless days that went nowhere. Toast for breakfast, walk to work, lay out his tools when he got to work, tuna fish sandwich for lunch, finish the day, work late, walk home, eat, TV, read the paper, sleep. This repetition had a tumbling effect - it seemed to all occur in the past.

Now, at sixty, he wakes and looks in the mirror, his face aged, wrinkled. His eyes not quite so bright anymore. Then the moment swallowed him, as if he sunk into all those years in that very second. It was a bottomless moment - he could even hear the growl of time - his heart ceased beating, his breath suspended as if the moment, like a great whale had engulfed him.

When his breath resumed, he wasn't sure if another decade had passed him by.

A Star in Time

"I can't make it like this no more," said Willy.

"You and me both," sighed Smith.

They sat on the floor across from each other, curled up in rags and blankets. They'd woken up in their usual hideaway: the long-abandoned wire spool factory that lined the street near the river. Through the grimy, shattered windows, they could see the city skyscrapers.

"Just a few more weeks of this, and I'm out of here," Willy said.

"I've been thinking the same," said Smith.

"Yes, sir," continued Willy. "I'm going to get a job, get married and go back to my old ways."

"This life ain't for everyone," agreed Smith.

"Why, I can see it now. Me all dressed up, walking to work with my briefcase, having bums polish my shoes," said Willy. Then his face softened. He continued, shaking his head. "Well, I'd toss those bums a couple of dollars."

"And right you should," said Smith.

"And what you going to do?" Willy asked. Smith rubbed his finger along a steel plank, as if trying to wipe away a secret message.

"I'm not sure what I'm going to do just yet," said Smith. "I'm thinking maybe I'm going to buy a big car, smoke cigars and drive around with pretty women."

"You old dog," said Willy, smacking his hands together. "You ain't going to settle down?" he asked, his mouth agape, struck incredulous by Smith's audacity.

"I ain't the settling down type," said Smith, his eyes suddenly distant. "I ain't never been able to be anywhere too long."

"Well, you been with me, old buddy, for at least a year," said Willy. Smith looked away. "And now I got used to you," Willy said, his eyes watering. He coughed a few times into his fist. Then he straightened up, grinned and spoke. "You ain't looking to split out of Dodge, you old dog you, eh?" Smith started to break a slight smile. "You got some riches you ain't telling me about?" asked Willy. "And after all this time?"

"I don't have nothing I didn't always have."

"Now, what does that mean?"

"I ain't got no riches, or nothing like that."

"Well, howdy do, Smith," said Willy, now serious. "If you ain't gonna tell me what you got, you ain't nothing."

"See here, Willy," started Smith. "What I've got is just a button that can take me places."

"That don't make no sense. Didn't we run out of whiskey? You hiding your drink?"

"I ain't had no drink."

"Then you just crazy," said Willy, spitting on the floor.

"Maybe I am. Maybe I am. If I weren't crazy, I wouldn't be out here with you, sleeping in dirty places, waking up with bugs crawling on my skin."

"That button you talking about. Is it shiny and gold like?" Willy asked. Smith's eyes widened in surprise. "Yeah, I found that thing you've been hiding in your pockets."

"Now you give it back to me," said Smith, realizing Willy must have slipped it from the pouch where he kept it.

"Lookee here, I ain't giving it back to you until you tell me what it is," said Willy.

"It's just a good luck charm. Something a special lady gave me a long time ago."

"Some special lady she must have been," Willy said. Smith agreed, shaking his head, never taking his eyes off Willy. "Where that lady from?"

"She was a special lady from where I'd grown up in the south."

"That right, Smith? They speak Egyptian or something like that where you'd grown up?"

"Naw, that's just a good luck charm. A pendant."

"Something going to happen when I open it?"

"Just give it here, Willy."

"Is it going to make me rich?"

"It ain't going to do nothing you want it to do, Willy."

"Is that right?"

"That's what I know."

"Well, I'm itching to see what magic that charm can do."

"I'm saying this for your own good," said Smith, sighing. "Hand it over." Willy shook his head no. "Please!" Smith begged. But Willy didn't yield.

Smith picked himself off the sooty floor, dusted his high-water pants and walked out of the dingy room. He shambled down the stairs and made his way to the street.

Willy walked over to the window and looked down to the street. He waved to Smith as if to say, "Don't be mad at me." Smith waved back goodbye.

A few hours later Smith returned. He trudged up the stairs to the ramshackle room where they'd lived for the past month. "Willy?" he called out. His voice echoed like a pipe clanging on a steel wall. No response. He felt as empty and hollow as the room itself. Smith looked down to Willy's usual spot. The gold button glittered, even in the black dust.

Smith reached down to pick up the button. He read the etchings on the gold. They were in a digital language, the language of his home planet. This pendant was hardly worth anything as a gold piece. There were moveable chambers on the pendant, like you'd see on a combination lock. In fact, if you pressed the moveable chambers just right, you dialed yourself to another galaxy millions of light-years away. If you pressed the wrong combination, while the button fell to the ground, you might get flung smack into an asteroid or get sucked into a neutron star and flung into a million little pieces, like so many bits of dirt in a great wind.

The Numbers Man

Smith walked into Monroe's Bar. He'd gone there a few times a week, now that he was in this little town. Being new in town, he'd sit at the bar, trying not to stand out too much. He had spoken to Billy, the bartender, every night he'd stopped in. Smith settled onto a barstool.

"The usual?" asked Billy.

Winking in agreement, Smith tilted his head and pointed at the Miller tap with his chin. Billy spun a fresh pint glass from the rack and pulled on the tap handle.

"How's it going tonight?" asked Smith.

"Yeah, good," said Billy. "Finished work?"

"That's why I'm here," said Smith.

"Well, if you're a betting man," said Billy, pointing to the chalkboard behind him showing the week's football games, "you might want to join the football pool." A bartender knows when someone›s lonely and might be looking for a way to get in on the action.

"Tell you the truth, I'm not a betting man," said Smith. Smith had overheard a few guys talking earlier that week about how Billy made a percentage of the bar's sports pool.

"Is that so?"

"And I don't know much about football," admitted Smith with a frown.

"You're joking," replied Billy, crossing his broad arms on his chest. His arms were covered with tattoos: a Celtic cross on a hill, Jesus's face with a teardrop of blood and two dragons swallowing each other's tails, their long, slender bodies wound in an infinite loop.

"Sadly, no," said Smith.

"What'd you drop in from another planet?" asked Billy, laughing.

"You might say so."

Now Billy heaved with laughter, his belly jiggling up and down. Despite his bloated stomach, his arms and chest bulged with muscles.

"Well, you think about it, and I'll be back," said Billy, lumbering away to help another customer.

As the night went on, Smith drank his pints quietly, looking up at the T.V. perched on the shelf over the bar. It was a Thursday night game, New York versus Dallas.

"So, you ready to wager ten bucks for the big cash prize?" asked Billy. Since Smith didn't say anything, Billy pulled out the week's lineup, showing the spread for each game. "See here, since Dallas is playing in New York, and New York has a better record so far, New York is the three-and-a-half-point favorite." Waiting for Smith to acknowledge, Billy paused. "Get it?"

"I think so," said Smith. "New York has to beat Dallas by more than three-and-a-half points, right?"

"Exactly," said Billy, trying not to sound condescending. He then went down the list with Smith, discussing each of the games. "Okay, so you're in?" he asked.

"Ten bucks?"

"Ten bucks gets you in for the week. Seventy-five gets you in for the season," Billy said. Smith plunked down seven tens and a five. Like most other people in the bar, Smith watched the game with rapt attention, except he was learning the rules as he watched. He slammed his fists down on the bar when his team dropped catches or missed tackles, mimicking the noisy crowd. He won that night. Dallas lost by ten points.

Smith returned to the bar on Sunday.

"How you looking in the pool?" Billy asked. Smith detailed his picks, showing that he was winning. Billy joked "See that! And you're not a gambling man? Pulling my leg." Smith took a long draft of the Miller as soon as the pint hit the bar. He noticed someone leaning over his shoulder. A woman.

"I see you know how to pick a winner," she said.

"Well, you know, I only—"

Reaching out her hand, she said, "Name's Claire. Claire Rodgers."

"Smith," he replied, wiping the beer froth from his upper lip.

"Smith what?"

"Smith. Just Smith."

"Mysterious, aren't we?" She looked him up and down, as if being inscrutable made him more handsome.

"Maybe I'm wanted in a few states," he said, smiling.

"Some people aren't wanted anywhere," she said, sliding onto the barstool next to him.

"Where you from?" she asked. "You ain't from around here." *She has a lopsided smile*, he thought. One eyelid closed more than the other. Pretty blue eyes. Dark, black, straight hair. Bangs. He told her he was from down south.

"You don't seem like a Southerner," she said.

"We're not all hillbillies. Some of us are just regular people."

She laughed. "You're cute for a wanted man."

They talked long after the game was over, Smith buying drinks all night. Claire was a football fan, too. "My ex was a Dolphins fan, so I watched my share of games," she said.

"What happened?" Smith asked.

"Some things just didn't work. It's a long story, kind of like your name."

"You want to get out of here?" he asked.

"What? Are you going to take me home and tie me up?"

"Only if you're lucky," he said.

They drove back to his place in separate cars. Claire stretched out on the couch, kicking off her shoes at the heels with the tips of her toes.

"This's a nice place."

"All the furniture came with the apartment."

"But where did you come from, really?" she asked, suddenly serious. "And what are you doing here?"

"I come from down south."

"Who says that? People name a city. They give their last name. They don't just arrive in a small town for no reason." She stopped speaking for a beat. "Are you in trouble of some kind?"

"Not exactly," he said.

"Well, look, I like you. But I don't like this talking around the bush," Claire said.

"It's hard for me to talk about."

"Comes a time a man's gotta be straight."

"What happened with the jokes?"

"Joking time's over now," she said.

"You're never going to believe me."

"Try me," she said, pulling out a cigarette. "You mind?" When he didn't say anything, she lit it up.

"Well, you see, I'm not a numbers man, and where I'm from, we talk in numbers."

"What does that mean?"

"I'm from far away," he said.

"How far?"

"What if I told you I'm from another planet?"

"I'd say that about makes sense," Claire said, "I only seem to like crazy men."

"I told you you'd think I was nuts," he said. "See, where I'm from, my planet, everyone is like one of your computers. We all have an incredible grasp of numbers, of technology."

"Is that why you're so good at the football scores?" she said playfully, as if going along with his game.

"You don't believe me?"

"I don't know, Smith. Sounds like a crock, like you're avoiding something."

"I'm not."

"Well then, why did you leave?"

"I'm not a numbers person. I'm a word person," he said. "I love poetry, language, stories. I'm learning about your kind. Your people are made up of stories."

"But you're so good at numbers."

"To be honest, I'm dumb at numbers compared to others from my planet. Humans just aren't very good."

She took a long drag on her cigarette, trying to weigh the truth of his words.

"So how did you get here?"

He pulled out a tiny, gold pendant inscribed with digital symbols. "See here. Just be careful. Don't play with it. Just look." He held it out in the palm of his hand. Claire pulled back a little, putting her hand over her mouth.

"Smith, that's just too much. This just can't be."

"Do you want to leave? I'd understand."

"I have to think this over."

"For what it's worth, I like you," he said.

"Well, I just don't know what this would mean."

He knew the look on her face. It was a look that said he was either cracked, or he was really from another planet ¾ and then what?

Smith knew that he'd have to move on. She wasn't the one. If she blabbed at the bar, no one would believe her, anyway. Smith was just another transient, they'd say. Another nut job. A drifter. And no one would remember him from Adam.

The Productions of Time

Smith arrived in a beach town after driving for a few hours towards the coast. He had a sudden urge to see the ocean. The ocean reminded him of looking out into space.

He found a winding road that led to a strip of shore. Some of the shoreline was private, marked off with signs and orange fencing. Other areas were public.

He parked the car and stepped out to stretch. It was early morning; the seagulls were circling the sky, cawing. Sunlight danced on the waves. There were bits of rocks and shells scattered along the shore. He walked down to the beach.

He took off his shoes and sat on the beach, digging his toes into the sand. The sand was cool and smooth. He looked out to the ocean. This world seems so vast and yet so tiny. Most people on this planet go their whole lives without realizing the vastness. Despite this, humans were complex. Though irrational, some had deep feelings and wrote glorified verse. Earthlings kill for their prophets and gods. His own kind were almost too perfect, made empty by their colossal minds. Those like him, who were more compelled by words and music, left for other places.

Smith saw a man walking toward him in the distance, his pants rolled up to his knees, holding his shoes in his hands. As the man came nearer, Smith could see his white beard and hair. The man had a deep tan.

"Beautiful, isn't it?" said the man.

Smith noticed that the man's eyes were emerald green. "Incredible," he answered. "Do you live around here?"

"I do now," said the man. "I retired a few years ago."

"Lucky, you get to wake up to this every day."

"I'm grateful to be near the ocean," said the man. He gazed out, as if the answer was somewhere out there. "But I would have preferred to enjoy this with my wife." Smith was silent. "She died two years ago, just as we both retired. We had planned to move to the coast, travel and live out the rest of our lives together."

"I'm sorry," said Smith.

"And you?" asked the man. "Did you come here to escape something? To find something?"

"Like you, I guess I came to find a place for me to fit in. I've been searching far and wide."

"I understand. An old retired professor doesn't fit in too easily, either. An old retired professor who lost his best friend and can't fall in love again."

"How long were you together?"

"Thirty years. We met in graduate school. She was smart, she was pretty, and she actually liked me," he chuckled.

"I guess I've never known anything quite like that. I've lived most of my life as a loner," said Smith.

"Well, a handsome young man like you should have no trouble finding someone."

"I'm complicated."

"I see. One of those," said the man. "I traded in 'complicated' for having my arms around Rosie every night. Sometimes it felt like I was holding onto the whole world."

"Do you regret it now?" asked Smith. He immediately wished he could take that question back. He was still learning about the depths of human irrationality.

"Not one bit."

A flock of seagulls flew overhead, cackling. The tide now rushed in, wafting a light spray of salt-perfumed air with it. Smith and the man watched the scene in silence. There was ocean as far as the eye could see. It was like a picture of eternity.

"Well, my young friend," said the man. "I guess I'll be heading on."

"Nice talking to you," said Smith. They didn't exchange names. Sharing confidences was too personal to spoil with names and particulars.

As the man walked away, he turned back around and said, "I don't regret any of it one bit," shaking his head knowingly.

Earth to Earth

Smith preferred earthlings because they sang and dreamt, even the murderers and thieves.

He drove across America, over the Rocky Mountains, in the canyons of Utah and into the California desert, seeking something. You might call it companionship. Making contact.

One night, at a camp site in the Mojave Desert, Smith met Dr. Oscar Gonzalez. Gonzalez's Harley Davidson was parked next to Smith's SUV.

"Nice bike," said Smith, whistling with pursed lips, the light from his campfire dancing on the shiny metal surface of the bike.

"She drives like a beauty," said Gonzalez, fiddling with the telescope he'd setup near his Harley.

Gonzalez had curly, grey hair. He was short, about sixty years old. He wore a checkered sports jacket that had suede patches on the elbows.

"What you looking at?" asked Smith.

"Saturn," replied Gonzalez, twisting the lens with his thumb and index finger. "Want to see?" he added.

Smith shook his head yes, looking the telescope up and down as he walked near it, intrigued by its strange design. He'd never seen anything like this telescope; it resembled a piece of antique furniture.

His eye now nestled into the lens chamber; Smith saw Saturn about the size of a penny in the eyepiece.

"Clear as a bell," said Smith.

Smith gazed for a minute or two, then he stepped back. As if unable to wait his turn again, Gonzalez resumed his position at the telescope.

"Where'd you get this thing?" asked Smith.

"Designed and built it myself," said Gonzalez. "Made it out of a dresser drawer, inserting a series of lenses and mirrors placed in just the right way to magnify objects as distant as planets." The dresser drawer was turned upside down on its head.

"She's even got her own limo," said Gonzalez, pointing to the wagon attached to his Harley. The words *Fermi's Paradox* were painted in firetruck red on the side of the wagon.

Crude, but clever thought Smith.

"Are you an astronomer?" asked Smith.

"I'm a mathematician," said Gonzalez, "but I'm also an amateur astronomer." For a moment, he looked at Smith. "I've always been interested in the stars and planets. I'm one of those people who measure and count."

"What do you mean?" asked Smith.

"My ex-wife said it was Asperger's, said Gonzalez," hardly looking up from the telescope.

"I can relate," said Smith.

"You're like that, too?" asked Gonzalez.

"In a way," answered Smith. "It's a long story."

"It's all relative," said Gonzalez.

Smith waited a few minutes to speak while Gonzalez operated the telescope. He could tell that Gonzalez loved turning the knobs and dials on the device he'd built. Earthlings had passion. They may not have been the best scientists, but they made up for it in pluck.

"Do you think you'll find a spaceman with that thing?" ventured Smith, laughing.

"Let's just say I have a nagging suspicion that given all those stars out there," said Gonzalez, adjusting the lens again, "there must be another planet that produced life. It might not be like Earth. Maybe it's an altogether different kind of planet and different kind of life."

"You mind if I have another look?" asked Smith.

"Be my guest," said Gonzalez. "I've been waiting a long time for someone to enjoy the view from this lens. I've had a lot of passers-by but no real takers." He paused. "Where'd you say you were from?"

"I'm from the south," said Smith.

"I thought I heard a hint of a Southern twang in your voice. Tennessee? Kentucky?"

"It's a long story," replied Smith. "Relatively speaking," he continued.

"My wife was from the south, too," said Gonzalez, like he was asking a question.

As Gonzalez stepped back from the telescope, he motioned for Smith to come take a look. Then Smith bent down and beheld Saturn once again. Beautiful Saturn, with its smooth surface and magical rings. Beautiful Saturn, he repeated to himself. Being someone from another galaxy, Saturn reminded him of Earth, like it was its cousin or just a close neighbor.

Then Smith noticed something. Something weird. He adjusted the telescope lens to focus in on an image he thought he saw orbiting the surface of Saturn. Upon closer inspection, he realized that the tiny image was none other than Gonzalez waving at him. He looked up from the telescope and saw Gonzalez, now standing only two feet away from him, waving at him. He looked back and forth, from the telescope to the person standing in front of him. He even noticed that

Gonzalez's movements synchronized with the waving image orbiting Saturn.

Then it all became clear.

Gonzalez opened his clenched hand, revealing something shimmering. Nestled in the palm of his hand, Smith saw a golden button.

"It's all relative," said Gonzalez, a broad smile on his face. "My wife was from the south, yes," continued Gonzalez. "But the south of what? It's all relative," repeated Gonzalez, laughing.

Smith starting chuckling, too. Then they reached out to shake hands and embraced.

Pale Leviathan

The heat had become unbearable that summer.

"Make it stop, daddy," Liddy's son, Torrin, said, as they walked home from school. The sun glared down with a vengeance, its rays like vicious lapping tongues. It seemed to Liddy that the sun was angry at the earth.

"I can't make it stop," said Liddy. "But we'll be home shortly. Mom will have the freezing air on." People had to get special solar powered freezing air units to maintain livable temperatures in their homes. The sun rained down relentlessly, as if hurriedly punishing the earth.

Holding Torrin's hand, Liddy felt the heat blasting his face, too.

"Please, daddy," said Torrin.

The shine beat down on his eyes, even with the sun goggles on. Without the goggles, you couldn't open your eyes, or your eyes teared and became blood shot.

When they got home, Torrin cried, the temperature so powerful it made his skin break out in red blotches.

"Rinse your eyes with cool water," his father said. Torrin stopped crying once the cool water hit his face.

As they prepared for dinner, Liddy lifted the canvass shade covering the window. Outside, the sky looked hazy and dense. The sun's rays rushed in like a swarm of bees, even though he just peeked out the window.

"I tell you not to do that all of the time, Liddy," said his wife, Kate, sighing. Kate had thin, black hair. Her face, normally pale, was reddened from the sun. Her cobalt-blue eyes were made bluer by the pronounced red skin color.

"Sorry, I know, I just feel so trapped."

Kate looked over at Torrin, who was playing a video game, to make sure he wasn't listening.

"We all feel trapped," she whispered. "The world keeps getting hotter and smaller. Before you know it, we're not going to be able to go out." Her face looked scared now. "And then what?"

Liddy knew she was right. He had a hard time shaking old habits. He grew up biking and hiking in the hills of Marin, California. He had moved to Flagstaff, Arizona to take a teaching position. It was hotter everywhere, but it was hottest in Arizona. Turning the news on would bring some terrible update almost weekly now: flooding, hurricanes, tornados. The tide of climate change was now crashing down upon us. Liddy taught English literature. He wasn't sure if teaching English was completely useless or the most important thing he could do.

"We're going to keep doing what we need to do, honey."

"I'm sorry," said Kate. "Come here."

They held each other closely. Some people, especially those that got lobster red, were more likely to get the new form of fierce cancer that was rapidly spreading. This new cancer, nicknamed 'The Solar Curse,' was taking thousands of lives every year. It literally burned through people, making their veins like rivers of fire. Their skin dried up and turned beet red, as did their eyes, all in a matter of months. Some died of dehydration; their mouths became parched, as if choking on ash.

After dinner, they turned on the cooling lights.

Liddy helped Torrin with his homework as Kate prepared the house for the evening cooldown, the coolant system now releasing recycled water used that day. The water froze the ground and the walls, generating fresh air and lowering the house temperature. Kate had been a geologist and was now a consultant to SunVeil, a company that developed innovative temperature coolant systems.

"Are we going away this summer?" asked Torrin, as he closed his books, now finished with his homework. "Last year we went to Iceland to see the geysers," he added, his eyes brightly glowing in the cooling lights.

"We'll see," said Kate. Last year was a good five degrees cooler on average. Adding up the increases in temperature, the world had jumped up about fifteen degrees, in some places almost eighteen.

"Please say yes, mom."

"Yes, maybe we can go to Greenland or Alaska," she agreed. Just the thought of Alaska felt cool. All she could think about these days was Christmas as a kid in New England. Frosted windows decorated with snowmen and Santa Claus. Staring up at the starry sky. Whenever she felt a wave of panic creeping up or heat flashes on her neck, she imagined the wind whirling around her house in December. The whistling used to scare her as a kid. She'd call her father and mother to her room to make them stop the whistling.

"Don't worry," her mother said. "It's just the wind."

"Maybe it's a ghost," said little Kate, her pretty blues welled up with tear drops.

"Mommy and daddy are here, sweetheart. We're downstairs. There are no ghosts. Go to sleep now." Her mother tucked her in again, now for the fourth time this evening. Kate fell asleep eventually, covered up to her eyes so she could see the ghosts if they came out.

After homework, Liddy read "Hiking in Alaska" aloud to Torrin. Reading about the pine trees and the cool, fresh lakes felt good to Liddy, too.

"Could we visit the places where the soil is still frozen?" asked Torrin.

"I'd like that, too," answered Liddy. "I'd like to walk on the frozen lakes, breathing cold air from my mouth." Torrin couldn't wait to be in the fresh Alaskan air, his face cooled by the icy breezes.

Liddy tucked Torrin in bed.

Later that night, Liddy felt the heat pushing in on the house. Even though they had the freezing air on and the coolant chilling the floors, the heat seeped in the cracks, bled into the atomic pores of the fortifications.

Kate was already asleep. Liddy didn't turn towards her. He was sweating; his body was pulsing with heat. He rolled on his back.

He could see the hot vapor, like a pitiless ghost, issuing from the ceiling.

Skies of Hell Flames

The Texas heat beats down on the lawn in front of the house. There is a scorching wind gently blowing the blades of inch-high grass. The grass is wet green, as if oil soaks through the surface to slicken the grass.

The sun's blaze doesn't reach the inside of the house. Along with the tarantulas and snakes, it's stopped at the front door.

A sign hangs in the kitchen that reads "God Bless This House." The walk-in kitchen is designed perfectly; its drawers are filled with corn cob holders, lime squeezers, eggbeaters, spaghetti servers. All silver. A wine rack nailed to the cabinet displays crystal wine glasses hanging upside down as if in a state of eternal crucifixion.

"We have to be ready by noon," says James. "My mom has the photographer for three hours only."

"I wish she'd given us more notice," says Natalie. Her face is red, her eyes half closed from too little sleep.

"She told us a week ago," says James.

"I need more time to schedule the hairdresser." She speaks looking into the mirror, combing her hair.

Buttoning his shirt, James looks into the mirror on the other side of the dresser drawer. His small, blue eyes sink into the puffed flesh around them. The fat from his neck swells out of the shirt.

"I don't know why your mother does this to me. She doesn't want me to look pretty," shouts Natalie.

Later that night they come back from the family photo session.

"Well, I guess the pictures came out okay," she says.

He nods.

"I'm just so tired. What with work, the kids and everything else," says Natalie, pouring wine into a large glass. The liquid makes a gurgling sound as she pours it.

"You're taking those pills. You're not supposed to mix them with alcohol."

She takes a long drink.

"I found another broken glass on the floor," he says. You get so drunk you don't remember dropping glasses on the floor. What if Johnny steps on a piece of glass?"

"I don't feel like talking about this," she says. "You don't know what the pressure at work is like."

"You're the one who wanted the high-paying job."

"We'd never get by on what you make."

Running into the kitchen, their little girl, Cindy, pulls on her mother's hand.

"Mommy, come see what Johnny has done."

The image of the broken glass flashes into James's mind.

"Mommy come now, Cindy repeats. Now louder, "Mommy."

"Okay, I'll come," she says, emptying the wine in one gulp.

Sitting at the kitchen table, James looks out the window across to the playground. It's still daylight. There is no one there. There's almost never anyone there. He needs to paint the fence around the house. It's getting to look worn. The heavy rain from last night left torn branches in the yard. The wind blew so strong it had rattled roofs, unlatched doors and broken windows.

He pours himself a scotch.

Returning back to the kitchen, Natalie fills up her glass with wine. Cindy sits next to her, wearing her princess pajamas. Johnny is now fast asleep in his bedroom upstairs.

"I said please watch the drinking," says James.

"It's not like you don't drink. You're the one who couldn't remember whether you brushed Cindy's teeth last night."

"It ain't easy being a manager at the auto shop. I may not have a fancy title, but it takes the life out of me."

"Mommy I want ice cream."

"Go get the ice cream," says Natalie to James, interrupting their conversation.

"It's too late for ice cream," says James.

"My little princess can have ice cream anytime," she says. "I buy it with my money." Her voice slurs as she speaks.

He gets up from his seat, walks to the freezer in the garage and gets the ice cream, rankled by his wife's comments. He puts the ice cream on the kitchen counter.

"Mommy, mommy, I want ice cream," says Cindy.

"I told daddy to get you ice cream," Natalie says sternly, staring now at James.

"Did you look at the counter?" he asks.

Natalie sees the ice cream, clapping her hands and licking her lips.

"Do you know mommy loves you," says Natalie.

Cindy looks at her mother silently.

"Do you know how much mommy loves you?" Natalie growls from the back of her throat.

"Leave her alone," says James. "She heard you. We all love you; don't you understand? We're all here together in this house. Ain't nobody leaving." His eyes well up with water.

"I'm going upstairs to take my makeup off now."

Then James and Cindy walk out to the porch.

"You see that star right there?" he asks. "That's the North Star, right at the center of the Big Dipper."

"Is it far away, daddy?"

"It's very far away."

"As far as the sun?"

"No, the sun is closer. In fact, Texas is closer to the sun than New York. That's why it's hotter here, raining hell flames down on us sometimes."

After talking for a while, they return back into the air-conditioned house.

"What brings you back in?" asks Natalie.

"Mosquitoes," says James.

"Did you tell her about the stars?"

James doesn't say anything. He fills his glass with scotch.

"Did you tell her about the stars? I want my daughter to be the smartest girl in the class. Do something useful with that education you had."

"That's enough," shouts James.

"I'm putting Cindy to sleep now, since I'll remember that I did it," she says.

"I hope you remember to clean up the broken glass," he counters.

Now, alone in the kitchen, James stares at the family pictures that adorn the walls. Pictures of Cindy in princess outfits. He is crying, but his face doesn't show it.

Later, husband and wife both on the couch, holding their drinks in the dark, they sit in silence.

Natalie clutches James's hand in hers. He squeezes it tighter.

Tomorrow's Ghost

Liddy woke that morning drenched in sweat. He could still smell the scent of his wife Kate on the warm sheets. She'd left to go to Canada for the International Climate Change Conference the night before.

While still in bed, he mulled over his recurring dream of being followed by an alien being. In his dreams, the alien's presence was protective. Sometimes his dreams were violently interrupted by another force. The other force was demonic in nature. It seemed intent on suffocating him. Nailing him shut into a coffin where he couldn't breathe.

Shaking his head, Liddy rubbed his eyes. *What's wrong with me? I have to get Torrin ready for school by myself today. And then head to work.*

He waved his hand near the sensor to turn on the solar powered light in Torrin's bedroom.

"Come on, kid. Rise and shine."

Torrin began to stir.

"Get yourself ready; come have breakfast, and I'll drop you off." Then they got dressed and ate.

Opening the door to the house, the flaming sunlight burst in like water breaking through a dam.

Liddy and Torrin ran to the electric car to escape the scorching winds. As they rushed toward the car, Torrin dropped one of his books.

"Go, go" said Liddy, motioning for Torrin to get into the car. Then Liddy reached down to pick up the book. It felt like a piece of hot iron. He pulled the book up by its pages, his fingertips burning just to touch them. There were puddles of sunshine on the ground; the light blasted his eyes, blinding him.

Opening the car door, Liddy jumped into the front seat then slammed the door shut and sighed, resting his hands on the dash.

Liddy looked at Torrin, his eyes watery, his chest heaving.

"Are you okay?" asked Liddy.

Torrin shook his head affirmatively.

"Daddy, they're saying we won't have school soon. That we'll attend school virtually," said Torrin, his voice cracking with worry.

"That might not be for a while," replied Liddy, still huffing, knowing it was going to happen sooner. This just couldn't go on, people running around, children scampering out of the sun, like the earth was on fire.

As a college professor, Liddy's lectures were given remotely. They could be recorded and cataloged. But kids needed the socialization. His couldn't have been the last generation to be socialized, to make friends in school, to play basketball in an outdoor court. What will tomorrow's world be like? Will people be trapped in their homes, caged in their rooms?

After school, later that day, Liddy picked up Torrin. They came home and did homework.

"Are all stars as powerful as our sun?" asked Torrin, after they finished.

"Our sun is a normal star. It's not what you would consider a powerful star. Though, of course, it is powerful."

"Will the sun exist forever?"

"No, the sun will one day implode, scientists say, pulling the planets apart when it does."

"When will that happen?"

"Not for millions of years," said Liddy. Though millions of years was far away, it still seemed final and dreadful.

"What will we do on the earth when the sun explodes?"

"We don't have to worry about that now," replied Liddy, knowing that Torrin was asking the right questions.

"I want to be a climate scientist like mom when I grow up," said Torrin.

"That's a good goal," said Liddy, moved by his son's earnestness. Only eight, and Torrin already showed great empathy for people, for the world.

"How long will I live?" asked Torrin, out of the blue.

Questions, always asking questions.

"Well, normal lifespan is about a hundred years," answered Liddy. "How long do you want to live? Do you want to live forever?"

"I only want to live forever if you and mommy are with me," said Torrin, innocently.

Liddy wiped the tear that welled in his eye.

That night, Liddy dreamed again about the alien. He didn't know what else to call it. The being's presence was comforting in the midst of his nightmares. Perhaps he was so addled from worry that his dreams became disturbed and turbulent. In his dream the alien spoke to him, but the words were garbled and distorted, like you'd hear on a short-wave radio that was just out of reach.

"I can bring you here," said a light-blue vaporous form. It looked more like a wrinkle in the air than a being.

"But where are you?"

"I am far away; I want to help you, to help others, escape," it said, its voice like ribbons of notes.

"How will you help me, or us?"

"There is a way. There are paths open."

"I don't know what that means," said Liddy.

"You will know," said the voice; then the dream ended.

The next day, Liddy and Torrin watched the news on the video screen while eating breakfast in the kitchen nook. The screen showed images of gigantic icebergs melting in the North Pole, their waters spilling into coastal cities, destroying everything in their wake. The video then zeroed in on the faces of some of the people. Despite the demolished houses, trees ripped down and streets turned upside down, there were smiles on the faces of the people. One man spoke to a reporter, saying that the icebergs melting was an act of God, bringing relief to the Nordic countries. The man's eyebrows were tinged with frost. The video showed people dancing in the streets among the rubble.

Kate arrived back from Canada the next day, just as Liddy and Torrin were preparing to have dinner.

"We missed you so much," said Liddy, after embracing his wife. Torrin rushed to his mother, hugging her by the waist.

Then they all sat down together, Kate's knapsack and luggage still piled on the kitchen floor.

Liddy could tell by the look on her face not to discuss the details of the conference. It might be too unsettling for Torrin to hear. With the daily images from the news video and lessons at school, it was already too much.

"How was Canada?" asked Liddy, trying to focus on something positive.

"Canada was beautiful," said Kate. The air was cooler and fresher in the Northern Rockies. "We went on a number of excavations in the mountains, testing the soil and collecting tree samples," she added, as her bright-blue eyes sparkled.

"How are they treating their American peers?" asked Liddy, knowing that there was growing tension between the United States and Canada and other international democracies. There had been an increasing number of American refugees fleeing to Canada. Some people even pleaded with the Canadian government to take their children, even if they couldn't stay in Canada. With climate change running amok in the United States, on top of a growing authoritarian government, the rest of the world began to look at the United States suspiciously.

"Well, they know that climate scientists certainly don't side with the current administration," said Kate. Then, she added, speaking to Torrin, "What did you learn about in school these last few days, honey?"

"We've been learning about the sun, about climate change, about how big the universe is," said Torrin.

"Those are tall subjects for a little man," said Kate, smiling, now holding Torrin's chin in the cup of her hands.

"I want to be like you when I grow up, mommy."

"That's so sweet, honey. You don't want to be like your dad?" asked Kate, now rolling her eyes at Liddy.

"I want to save the world, mommy, like you."

"Daddy's saving the world in his way, honey."

That night, Liddy again dreamt about the alien. First the blue-ribboned form, then the garbled voice.

"You're back," said Liddy.

"Yes, I came for you."

"You came for me?"

"To take you to our world." Its voice whirred and whizzed, the syllables sometimes separated in time, but sometimes doubling, like two voices speaking at once.

This was the first time the alien said the word "our."

"Where is your world?"

"It is very far away."

"How far away?"

"We are so far away, you could never fly to us in a machine of any kind."

105

"How long would it take us to get to you?"

"It would take sixty thousand years by conventional travel methods."

Suddenly, Liddy felt like he'd had this conversation before.

"Sixty thousand years by conventional methods?" asked Liddy.

"Remember, just like we had talked about before," said the alien.

"We've had this conversation?" asked Liddy.

Now, ignoring his question, the alien reached out his hand.

"I need you to take my hand," said the alien.

"What will happen?"

"When you take my hand, I will pull you into my world. You see, this is how we travel. In dreams."

"I'm dreaming, that's right," said Liddy. He had had a few lucid dreams before.

"Yes, you're dreaming. Remember how you used to say that you have to live your dreams?"

"I used to say that to Torrin when he was a little boy."

Now a radio whir roared, as if from inside a gigantic subway station.

The alien held out his hand. Liddy reached toward the hand. Their touching set off a series of electrical sparks. Liddy found himself in a spinning tunnel; a cyclone of swirling color swarmed around him, rotating and turning. He held the alien's hand tightly. Whatever was happening, whether he was dreaming or not, he felt at peace. Somehow the presence of this being seemed to fill his heart with love. It reminded him of how he felt holding his father's hand.

After tumbling, his body shuddered and pulled; he was set free, then floated gently, his body slowly descending to the ground, like a bird that landed. Liddy looked around at the sky in this world. It was magnificent. There were so many stars, but these stars seemed closer and brighter. There were gigantic swatches of color across the sky, like the yoke of the galaxy had oozed out of its membranous enclosure.

Now, looking down from the sky, he noticed that he was still holding the hand of the alien.

They looked into each other's eyes.

"You look just as I remembered," said the alien. Its voice was no longer travelling over great distances. It was right in front of him.

Liddy knew the face in front of him.

"Who are you?" asked Liddy, confused about who it was he was looking at.

"We travel through dreams to cover the expanse of space."

"I'm not sure I understand," said Liddy. "Am I dreaming? Is this real?"

"I am who you think I am," said the alien.

Liddy's eyes filled with water. They joined both hands now, glancing into each other's eyes.

"And now, we have to go get mother," said the alien.

Storytime

"What should I read to you tonight, Pflx?" said Pflx's mother, Twlf, pointing to the translucent dome that covered their house.

"I want this one, Mommy," said Pflx. Her mind read his telepathically. Tonight, she would read to him the story of the blue-green world.

"So, you want to hear about Earth? How lovely," said Twlf, silently. Her opalescent eyes beamed like stars with excitement.

"Yes, Mommy." He paused, then asked, "Is it special?"

"Well, all of our stories are special. So yes, Earth's story is special, too. Wonderful. And sad."

"Does it have a happy ending?" he asked, his face now showing concern. After all, he was going to sleep. He didn't want bad dreams.

"Like many of the stories, this one is still in progress."

"Well," he said, making a sad face, "I guess you should tell me this one, now that I've asked." Now, secretly, he wanted to hear it, curious as to what she meant. Maybe there would be terrible monsters in this tale.

She took a deep breath and then began the story.

"On Earth, so many billions of years ago, life began, like life on our ancestors' planet began."

"Our ancestors aren't from this planet?" asked Pflx, again.

"No, our ancestors are from another universe. They managed to escape a universe that was imploding and then colonized the planet we now live on."

He was very proud that his ancestors journeyed across universes and that they were incredibly ancient.

"Can I continue?" asked Twlf.

"Yes, Mommy."

"Believe it or not, great monsters, called dinosaurs, once roamed Earth."

"What did they look like?" he asked.

Twlf showed him a holographic image of a dinosaur from her own mind.

Pflx's eyes opened in amazement.

Twlf then streamed a condensed history of the earth – from the Precambrian explosion of life to the death of the dinosaurs – into Pflx's mind. She then twirled the evolution of all Earth species on a beam of refracted crystal light.

"These monkeys are the smart ones on the planet?" asked Pflx.

"They are among the smartest, yes," answered Twlf.

"Why do you say, 'among the smartest?'"

She cast a swirl of light that raced through the history of humankind up until the great atomic wars.

"That's scary."

She shook her head, agreeing. Then she presented the more recent history of cities flooding and burning.

"And how does it end, Mommy?"

"See the plants here?" said Twlf.

Pflx nodded.

"These plants have the power to swing the door of time open."

"Like our space spice?"

"Indeed, like our space spice." And now, together, they envisioned how oceans can sing. How trees store time in their roots. Together they saw how rocks and water were made.

"When they discover that the rivers have songs, they realize that everything is made of space spice."

"Why is it so difficult for them to see this?"

"Ah, there is the mystery. Even our ancestors fought to the death at one time. They only learned after they had nearly wiped out our species and destroyed our planet. Then they found the plants that make the spices. The plants helped them sing across the galaxies."

"Will the people from Earth ever learn?"

"Maybe they will."

"Can't we help them?"

"They have to experience the moment of awakening."

Pflx looked confused.

"When they have the moment of awakening," added Twlf, "they will be one with all of us."

"You mean all of the astronomic beings?"

"Yes, all of the astronomic beings. It has happened many times over since I was a little girl."

"How does it happen?" asked Pflx. He loved to hear his favorite stories over and over.

"When a race of beings is awakened," she said, smiling, her eyes twinkling like stars, "we all feel a warmth inside. The great songs are heard throughout all of the universes."

Pflx stared off into a dream world.

"Should I sing one of the songs to you?"

"Yes, I want to hear the song."

Now Twlf hummed one of the songs. The song sounded like a million voices coiled together in unison. It was like an entire history of beings singing at once. Some of the voices were joyous; some of the voices cried, but beautifully. The song made anyone who heard it see visions. There were pictures of tree roots wrapping around a planet, protecting it in a loving way. Pflx also saw finned creatures swimming in blue oceans and skies, opening wide to breathe in flocks of colorful birds. Pflx flew with the birds, feeling a cool wind on his face. Suddenly, he was sleeping and passed into deep dreaming.

Twlf gave Pflx a kiss on his forehead, tucking him into bed.

"Sleep tight, my love," she said, slowly dimming the night light to black.

Acknowledgements

Even this little book has taken a lot of people to bring it into the world.

Thank you to the editors at Mad Swirl: Johnny Olson, Tyler Malone, and Michael Clay for their innovative and open spirit and for publishing some of the stories in this collection. Grateful for my friends Michelle Reale and Chad Frame at Ovunque Siamo, who are also amazing poets, for believing in my writing. Thanks to Marianne Szlyk and Ryan Quinn Flanagan, two other fine poets, for your constant support. Thanks to my friend and fellow writer at the Red Hook Star Revue, Mike Cobb for your inspiration. Appreciate Rebecca Bauman for your reading and review. Grateful for Susan Kaessinger, my friend and creative co-conspirator, for your many readings, edits and suggestions. A deep bow of gratitude and thanks to my wife, Arielle, for often reading early drafts of my work and providing important insights.

And thank you to the team at Apprentice House: Kevin Atticks, Kelly Lyons, Kelley Chan, Mackenzie Britt and Eric Boyd. I've appreciated all of the hard work and sweat it took to help produce this book.

About the Author

Mike Fiorito is an Associate Editor for Mad Swirl Magazine and a regular contributor to the Red Hook Star Revue.

Mike is the author of *Call Me Guido* published by Ovunque Siamo Press. He is also the author of *Freud's Haberdashery Habits* published by Alien Buddha Press.

Mike lives in Brooklyn, NY with his wife and two boys. He is currently working on a novel.

Apprentice House Press
Loyola University Maryland

Apprentice House is the country's only campus-based, student-staffed book publishing company. Directed by professors and industry professionals, it is a nonprofit activity of the Communication Department at Loyola University Maryland.

Using state-of-the-art technology and an experiential learning model of education, Apprentice House publishes books in untraditional ways. This dual responsibility as publishers and educators creates an unprecedented collaborative environment among faculty and students, while teaching tomorrow's editors, designers, and marketers.

Outside of class, progress on book projects is carried forth by the AH Book Publishing Club, a co-curricular campus organization supported by Loyola University Maryland's Office of Student Activities.

Eclectic and provocative, Apprentice House titles intend to entertain as well as spark dialogue on a variety of topics. Financial contributions to sustain the press's work are welcomed. Contributions are tax deductible to the fullest extent allowed by the IRS.

To learn more about Apprentice House books or to obtain submission guidelines, please visit www.apprenticehouse.com.

Apprentice House
Communication Department
Loyola University Maryland
4501 N. Charles Street
Baltimore, MD 21210
Ph: 410-617-5265
info@apprenticehouse.com • www.apprenticehouse.com